RAZ
BERI

With thanks to Inclusive Minds (the CIC supporting and championing inclusion and diversity in children's books) for introducing us to Kay Channon through their network of Authenticity Advocates.

RAZ BERI

MATT STEPHENS

Firefly

First published in 2024
by Firefly Press
25 Gabalfa Road, Llandaff North, Cardiff, CF14 2JJ
www.fireflypress.co.uk

A CIP catalogue record of this book is available from the British Library.

ISBN 978-1-915444-61-5
ebook ISBN ISBN 978-1-915444-62-2
This book has been published with the support of
the Books Council Wales.

Typeset by Elaine Sharples

Printed and bound by CPI Group (UK) Ltd,
Croydon, Surrey, CRO 4YY

1.

Boring and Interesting, Horrible and Amazing

School today was … interesting. Well, some of it was AMAZING; some of it was HORRIBLE; some of it was very, very INTERESTING. And of course, most of it was seriously BORING. It is still school, after all.

Let's start with the BORING, get it out of the way: the Tudors and the Stuarts; stylistic conventions of non-fiction; acids, bases and alkalis; converting metric and imperial measurements; teacher after teacher going on and on and on … interested? Then you're reading the wrong book. Is there the tiniest chance that I'm going to need any of that stuff in my adult life? Really?

I certainly don't need it in my teenage life and yes, I am, amazingly, several days into my teenhood: Billy Turpin, thirteen last week. A nation rejoiced. Well, a tiny corner of Willesden Junction, north-west London did anyway. I'll tell you about the living hell that was my party later.

For now, let's tackle the AMAZING. Registration this morning: dull, standard, not amazing at all. Mr Balotelli, our group tutor: tall, dull, standard, not amazing at all, but *nice*. I like Mr Balotelli. He doesn't *mock*, like Mr Moore and Ms Do Nascimento; he doesn't *bore*, like Mr Lawrenson, Miss Savage, Mrs Claridge and the rest; he doesn't *shout*, like Misters Marsh and Bowles. I'll come back to *all* of them…

Mr Balotelli said, 'Listen up everybody, you will not believe what is going to happen in two weeks' time…'

Some of the kids, like me, looked up and gave him our full attention. I'm generally good in class, always quiet, and definitely not cool. The 'cool' kids, led by (The Evil) Rio, yawned and chatted and sniggered and stared at the ceiling. Rio looks and dresses like a model. He ran his hand through his shiny black hair and looked at his mobile. Mr Balotelli is scared of Rio and doesn't tell him off for it. If I looked at my mobile in class, it would be confiscated.

'Well, if you're not interested…' said Mr Balotelli. 'I can easily find some other work for you to do when the captain of the England football team comes into school.'

OMG. Even Rio and his followers were listening now.

'What?' said Rio. 'Shut up! You don't mean Danny Cash?'

Mr Balotelli nodded his balding head and smiled his sad smile.

Danny Cash: my absolute hero. Incredible, amazing, awesome. I had twenty-three pictures of him on my bedroom wall. And I wanted more. The great Danny Cash: captain of England and captain of Earl's Court FC. My team. My passion. My bedroom is painted in the ECFC colours: yellow and blue, like Brazil. My duvet is yellow and my pillowcases are blue. I've got pictures of the whole squad on my wall, but Danny Cash was the *star* by a mile. Still is. He's strong and stocky with a cuboid head (wow, I used a word that I learned in school – maybe it's not all completely useless) and has more talent in his left foot than the whole Manchester United squad put together.

'Danny Cash?' said Rio. '*The* Danny Cash is coming here?'

'That's right, Rio,' said Mr Balotelli. '*The* Danny Cash is coming to our school. And not just Danny Cash, Gary Reed and Nicky Dulgence are coming too. They'll be running a training session in double PE on Wednesday the tenth.'

Gary Reed and Nicky Dulgence are Danny

Cash's Earl's Court and England teammates. They're awesome too. Just not *quite* so awesome. I've got twelve pictures of Nicky Dulgence on my wall and nine of Gary Reed.

Mr Balotelli grinned while the class just went nuts. Kids were jumping out of their seats, whooping, grabbing each other, saying things like 'wicked' and 'sick' and 'omigod'.

I was nearly making the right noises myself too, but no one wanted to hug or high-five me. They never do these days.

Rio said, above the commotion, 'Mr Balotelli, sir, how come? How comes we got England players coming into our class?'

Mia, the new girl, was smiling quietly. Mr Balotelli walked over to her, put his hand on her wheelchair and said to the class, 'You might want to reflect for a moment on Mia's surname.'

I'd already been reflecting on Mia's lovely dark brown eyes, which was something of a new experience for me.

Mia smiled and simultaneously hissed, 'Don't touch my wheelchair, sir.'

Mr B went red and quickly removed his hand. No one else noticed. They were thinking about the new girl's name.

'What is it?' said (Horrible) Hisham, Rio's mate. 'Cash. Mia Cash, like Danny Cash ... noooooo.'

'Yeeeeees,' said Mia.

She's so gutsy. So not like me. She's new but she speaks up in front of the class, answers teachers back, stands up to anyone. Even Rio. You know, if she *could* stand.

Mia said, 'My Uncle Danny would do anything for me.'

She grinned some more while the class went crazy, all over again. Kids were whirling in each other's arms. Another of Rio's disciples, (Lame Brain) Liam, grabbed Mia's wheelchair from behind and spun her around in a circle. Mia's face turned scary as she reached behind her and grabbed Liam's kneecap. You could see the tips of her fingers digging in behind the bone. Liam's eyes opened wide.

'You let go of my chair NOW,' said Mia, 'or you never play football again.'

'Sorry Mia, sorry Mia,' said Liam. Rio laughed so everyone followed suit. Including me, damn it.

Rio makes my life a misery; I can't believe we used to be friends at primary school. Just a year or so ago. Before he learned to be 'cool'. Before he learned that hanging around with me was the opposite of cool.

Everyone followed his lead – they always do – and here I am, Billy-No-Mates.

'That's OK, Liam,' said Mia. 'As long as you understand that if I want you to move my wheelchair, I'll ask you.'

Liam nodded and then nodded some more.

'Do you have anything else, Liam, that you'd rather wasn't grabbed hold of and twisted through 360 degrees?' Mia had pulled her wheelchair around so she could glare at him.

Liam stared stupidly. Grinning, Rio said, 'Bruv, this is where you say, "yes Mia".'

Liam nodded again. He seems to be pretty good at that.

'I'm glad we understand each other,' said Mia, letting go. Wow, coolage.

She really is something.

'OK, settle down everybody please,' said Mr Balotelli. 'I need you to line up for assembly now and start thinking about how we can prepare for our famous guests. We'll discuss it in geography this afternoon.'

Mr Balotelli takes us for geography as well as being our group tutor. Normally it's about meanders, scree slopes and population density. Talking football would be one major improvement.

So that was the AMAZING. Shall we do INTERESTING or HORRIBLE next? Ah stuff it, let's get HORRIBLE out of the way…

The line at the door was buzzing. I couldn't join it because there were chairs in the way and no one had remembered to move them for me. Oh yeah, didn't I mention? I use a wheelchair too. I've got cerebral palsy. Cerebral palsy, or CP, is caused by brain damage as a tiny child or unusual development in the womb. Millions of people have it. It causes problems with muscles and co-ordination. With me, I find it really hard to use my legs. Also, when I talk, it comes out sounding funny. Kind of laboured and squeaky, like I'm an idiot or something. I'm not. Like I don't know what I'm talking about. I do. The thoughts I have are as good as anyone's. Better even. It's just when I express them, I sound like a cartoon character so I hate speaking up.

I was left behind. Again. The class all headed off to the science block. Mr Balotelli saw my problem and cleared the way.

'Hurry up now, Billy. You'll be late.'

'Yes, sir.'

All through the morning, no one talked about anything but football and the famous players we had visiting. At break time, everyone was playing football. Even some of the teachers. There were games springing up left, right and centre and I was desperate to be part of one. I hung around the edge of the biggest. Obviously, it was the one Rio and his mates were playing. Obviously, that was a stupid idea.

The ball ricocheted off (Sweaty) Scott's knee and bounced towards me. I caught it and everyone cheered. That was such a good feeling. It made me bold; it made me stupid. It made me say, 'I know, maybe I could be in goal.'

'What?' said Rio. 'What did you say, mong?'

'Mong' means Mongol. A horrible term for someone with Down's Syndrome. I don't even have Down's Syndrome. I wanted to tell them but I didn't. It's a genetic condition and when they say it, they're just showing their ignorance.

I felt my confidence draining fast but I managed to repeat myself, 'Maybe I could be in goal.'

'Mehbeh uh cuh beh in goo,' squeaked Rio and his mates all fell about laughing.

Was Stephen Hawking stupid? He hardly spoke 'normally'. In Mrs Robson's class, all those years ago, Rio used to look after me, play with me, beat up the kids that tried to tease me. Until he decided it was social death, hanging out with a 'spaz'.

'Spaz'. That one really hurts. It's an abbreviation for 'spastic'; a word no one uses anymore. No one decent, anyway. It was supposed to be a medical word, but now it means contempt, it means hate. It means I'm less than human.

'Do one, spaz-bag. You're taking up space.'

'Mehbeh uh cuh beh in goooo,' said Hisham and the laughter started up again. I felt the tears welling. My arms work fairly well – a bit shaky but fairly well. I threw the ball back, turned myself around and started wheeling away as quickly as I could. Away from the laughter.

Why are they like this?

I get this stuff all the time. It kills me. Having cerebral palsy isn't horrible; it's just me, and lots of other people. Being treated like that, like a half-human. That's HORRIBLE.

Most of the girls in my class think I'm 'cute' which isn't quite so bad, I guess. They go, 'ahh, bless' on the rare occasions that I open my mouth. At least they're not being vile to me like some of the boys are but, to tell the truth, I could do without them looking down on me. I mean, I know I'm in a wheelchair and all but you know, metaphorically. Blimey, another word I learnt at school. First 'cuboid', now 'metaphorically'. What's going on?

The thing with the girls is that I'm not really human to them either. To the boys I'm a 'mong' or a 'flid' or a 'spaz' – all cruel words. We've done 'spaz' and 'mong' already. 'Flid'? I had to ask my nan the first time someone called me that. It comes from Thalidomide; a drug that caused awful physical problems in new babies back in the last century. It's nothing to do with my condition. It's just another way of telling people they're less than.

To the girls I'm someone to fuss and cuddle when they're bored, or to push from lesson to lesson when they want to show how caring they are. More of a plaything really. All I want is to be treated normally. With respect and like a human being. Is that too much to ask? When Danny Cash comes, will it just confirm their prejudice or will it give me the chance to show them the real Billy Turpin?

Mia's only just joined this school but she sees how the other kids treat me. She doesn't follow them. Mia doesn't patronise me; she doesn't call me names. She doesn't do any of that stuff. Mia thinks for herself and doesn't care what other people think. Yeah, I never thought I would say this about a *girl* but Mia is seriously INTERESTING.

2.

Happy Birthday, Billy

Nicky Dulgence played a trademark, fifty-metre ball to me and the crowd gasped as I controlled it perfectly on my thigh, spun and took off down the wing. Old Trafford was packed with over seventy-five thousand rabid Manchester United fans. They do *not* like losing but they could only look on in awe as I sliced through their mega-expensive defence. Cutting inside one, then another, then another red-shirted superstar, I seemed to have the ball velcroed to my boot. Danny Cash screamed for me to cross but instead, I turned my back on the last defender, flicked the ball over both of our heads and left him on his backside as I deftly ran past him and volleyed the ball into the bottom corner from twenty metres out. Even the partisan home fans could only rise in acclaim at my genius.

Pursued by my teammates, I sprinted around the back of the goal, waving my yellow shirt in the air. I know it's an automatic booking but after a career-changing piece of skill like that, it was worth it.

There was only a minute left; there was no coming back for United.

Using my shirt as a flag, I raised my arm and turned a slow circle to acknowledge the crowd. I became conscious of the stare of a solitary canine eye, boring a hole into my Xbox world, leaving it in tatters.

I put my arm down. I put the controller down. Old Trafford quickly turned back into a little bedroom in a little flat in a little corner of Willesden Junction.

'What are you looking at?' I said to Nettle, my dog.

Billy Turpin, superstar, morphed back into Billy T. 'Billy the Flid. Smell on Wheels.'

Nettle is not much bigger than a guinea pig and she's more black hair than anything else. She's got three legs and one eye. Nettle looks like something a proper dog might cough up and yet, somehow, goodness knows how, she's totally cool. She stood on her hind legs and pawed at my knees with her one front leg.

'C'mon,' I said, patting my thigh and Nettle jumped up onto my lap. She didn't smell so good, bless her. I tried not to think about what she might have been rolling in.

My hands are a little too shaky for a standard computer keyboard, so I've got one designed for my needs. Each key is about three centimetres wide. It's great and I use it loads, especially when I'm chatting to my online friends, and I've got plenty. I use all the latest social media but I also use Facebook so I can see what stuff my mum's posting. Online, my voice is the same as anyone else's. Online I can talk about my CP or not. You can be whoever you want online. I love it because I don't have to worry about people laughing at me. I can just be me.

Sometimes Nettle barks at the screen and her solitary front paw jumps up and down on the keyboard. It's brilliant; I've got the world's only typing dog. She barked and spelled out:

dde dde

I said, 'Clever girl, but you need a little help with your spelling.'

I rubbed her head. She's the best dog.

You know I don't like talking because I've got such a funny-sounding voice? Well, Nettle doesn't care. I guess even my breathy squeak is better than her deranged yipping. I tell Nettle *everything*. Every last painful detail, in fact, especially the painful details. She never judges or mocks or interrupts. She listens, intently: head cocked; solitary eye fixed upon my mouth; desperately trying to get meaning from my words. Sometimes I really think that she understands.

I told her about what had happened yesterday, when Rio and Hisham were so nasty to me. It was one of those painful stories. But it wasn't finished…

I had turned around from the football match and started my escape when Mia rolled her wheelchair in front of mine.

I looked down at the ground as Mia gave me the full power of her stare.

'Where the hell do you think you're going?' she said.

It was the first time she had ever spoken to me.

'Are you gonna let them get away with that?'

'I can't play football, can I?' I said. 'Who am I kidding?'

'Of course you can, watch this.'

Toerag Tyreece was running down the wing with the ball. Mia swung her wheelchair into his path and sent him tumbling. She scooped up the ball saying, 'I can't use my feet so it can't be handball, can it?'

Rio looked amazed and just nodded. Mia looked up and slung a perfect pass into Liam's path. He couldn't miss the goal and he didn't.

'That ain't fair,' said Tyreece.

'What,' said Mia. 'Being made to look stupid by a raspberry?'

I couldn't believe it. 'Raspberry' is the latest insult. It's Cockney Rhyming Slang. It's from 'raspberry ripple' which rhymes with 'cripple'. Lovely. Rio and his mates reckon it's *so* funny. Often, they just blow a raspberry as I go by, then nearly wet themselves laughing. They wouldn't dare do that with Mia. Anyway, she's stolen their insult and claimed it for herself. How cool is that?

'You can't argue, Ty,' said Rio. 'Hey Mia, you wanna play?'

'Nah,' said Mia, leaving Rio looking snubbed. She turned to me. 'You gonna be a spaz all your life?'

'You can't call me that,' I said.

'I can if that's how you act,' she said. 'I know you've got CP like me but that's not what I'm talking about.'

I said, 'I can't do what you did.'

'What, you can't wheel your wheelchair? You can't throw a ball? I've just seen you do both those things before running away with tears in your eyes because the horrid boy said something horrid to you. Horridly. Bloody hell, Billy, stand up like a man, or sit down like one at least.'

'You swear too much, Mia.'

'No, Billy. You don't swear enough.'

She was wrong but I couldn't argue with her. At least she was talking to me.

I thought about what Mia had said and I tried swearing at Nettle now I was home. I looked her in the eye and said a really unpleasant word that would get me into so much trouble at school. Nettle just sneezed. I said it again; she sneezed again and banged her head on my armrest. It felt cruel, somehow.

My mum called from the kitchen, 'Billy, your tea's ready.' And my heart sank.

My mum's cooking is stuck in the early stages of development. She hasn't found the happy medium yet between raw and carbonised. Oh, good grief, there's another word I learned at school.

'Coming, Mum.'

We live in the ground floor flat of a low-rise block, so it's easy for me to get around. There are no stairs and I have easy access to outside because I can use the ramp. Sometimes it means pushing my wheelchair through some really gross stuff outside the flat but it's worth it because it means I can walk Nettle by myself. As long as people haven't parked their car up on the pavement and blocked my way. I love it; I'm just another dog walker then and other dog owners talk to me normally. Nettle likes our walks too. She likes eating the gross stuff, the dirty dog.

I pushed myself into the kitchen with the hairy little dog still on my lap.

'That dog can walk by herself, you know,' said Mum.

'She's disabled too, Mum.'

'She's got one more functioning leg than me, Billy, and three more than you. She's got a mind like a rattrap and if your nan was still alive, bless her, she'd say, "that dog's got the evil eye". I'm not surprised you were swearing at her just then.'

I blushed. 'No, I wasn't. I mean, I didn't mean it. I think she's really cute. I was just … trying something out.'

'I don't even want to know,' said Mum.

I love my mum and I love Nettle but it has to be said, they had conspired to ruin my birthday party last weekend. I told you I'd come back to that didn't I…?

Let's start with the food: 'You can't go wrong with burgers,' said Mum. It turns out you can. Especially if you cook them until they are blackened disks that shatter in your mouth. I did the cocktail sausages so they were barely incinerated at all. Obviously, Nettle jumped up onto the table and gave them a thorough savaging.

I also made a 'medley' of dips. Well, I think we can all agree that the introduction of a dog's backside does little for a garlic hummus; taramasalata is generally at its best when it hasn't been scraped off the kitchen floor; and the next time I make a spicy Mexican salsa, I will definitely try to make sure it doesn't induce screams, tears and vomiting within seconds of entering the mouth. I don't even want to think about my cake.

It was a makeover party. I know it's not terribly 'masculine', but I only had girl guests coming. The boys at school who aren't actively horrible to me, just try to pretend that I'm not there. They can't be seen talking to me so I don't have any male friends at school. I don't really like girls that much (at least I didn't before Mia came along), but the thought of me, Mum and Nettle sat in an empty room with our party hats on really was too sad to contemplate.

I just want some mates but apparently they don't want me so, 'girly' party then: five select female 'friends' wondering what on earth they'd got themselves into. Chantelle, Shanika, Shannon, Jaz and Maysoon were pretty keen at first. Before we'd had time to work on them. They poured in through the front door in a flurry of glamour and glitter, in a cacophony of shrieks and squeals and alien odours. They fussed over me in my party finery: 'Oh loooook, bless. Isn't he just adorable?' They eyed each other up to see who had the best party gear on. Maysoon did the 'mwa, mwa' kissing thing on my cheeks so the rest all did the same until I looked like a four-year-old who'd found his mum's make-up box. Then Shannon got a tissue and started wiping the lipstick from my blushing cheeks. Jaz tied a sparkly gold bow around Nettle's neck. Nettle slithered under a chair and glared.

Kerry, the makeover party lady, was smiley and blonde. She knew what she was doing. She came well-armed with a karaoke machine, a foot spa, make-up, glitter tattoos, hair extensions, nail art sets, Botox … I made up the last one. In short, everything a football-mad teenage lad could wish for.

Chantelle and Shanika and Shannon and Jaz and Maysoon fell upon the poor woman like jackals on a baby antelope. I was happy; I was sitting back and looking on with detached amusement as they squabbled and snapped over scraps. For a while.

You know, I really do need to start thinking things through. Once they couldn't stick or plait or cleanse or scrape or smear another millimetre, they turned their attentions on me. Nettle had escaped already, no doubt to throw up half-digested cocktail sausages somewhere private. I didn't stand a chance: I was engulfed by a giggling gang of over-made-up girls, battling under the weight of glitter, nail jewellery and eyelash extensions.

It was no contest. My already straight hair was further straightened; my fingernails were daubed in ten different colours and four types of glitter; I can't keep my feet still because of my CP so my toenails were mostly untouched but great gaudy streaks of nail varnish ran up my feet; my lips shone with raspberry-flavoured gloss; my terrified eyes were ringed with thick gloops of electric-blue mascara; a series of stick-on diamonds made their way up my left cheek like the plastic ducks used to on my nan's sitting-room wall. That's when my mum saved me from further humiliation by saying, 'Karaoke time!' At least I thought she had.

Karaoke is great fun. I'm a little shy but I love karaoke. I can sing better than I can talk. It's old-school and retro – it's the best laugh. When the machine works. When it plays at the correct speed. Ours was slow. I mean slooooooooooow. Taylor Swift sounded like a man. A very drunk man. K-pop classics sounded like they should be played at funerals. My party was starting to feel like one.

We finished the party with the food. I've told you about the food. It didn't cheer us up any.

My mum drew the curtains and turned off the lights, saying, 'Time for the birthday cake'.

Oh God, it was a vile creation that had taken Mum

the best part of a day. She meant well. She'd baked a blue sponge and a yellow sponge and cemented them together with blue icing. The whole thing was encased in a thick layer of gloopy yellow icing with ECFC written in blue on the top.

We saw the glow of the candles as Mum walked through the door with the cake. Kerry and the painted girls sang 'Happy Birthday' to the painted boy like they wanted to die.

Mum said, 'You can blow out the candles love, but I think Nettle might have got to the cake first…'

On my eleventh birthday, my mum got a cake from the supermarket. It was football-shaped. Me and the other boys (all boys, including Rio! Liam!) had just had the best time of our lives. Mum told us that we needed a new fence in the back garden and that the old one had to be destroyed. We didn't need telling twice. They jumped on it, I rolled my wheelchair over it, they snapped slats over their knees, I snapped slats over my wheelchair arms. We sweated, we laughed, we shouted… We reduced it to matchwood, then stuffed our faces with football cake, fizzy drinks, sausages, iced biscuits… No one wanted to leave.

When Rio's mum came to pick him up, he looked me in the eye and said, 'BEST. PARTY. EVER!'

That was before secondary school. Before Rio realised it was cooler to bully me than to be my friend.

The morning of my party this year I had a message saying,

crappy birthday spaz – mite b yr last –
will be if u try an ruin r footie games

It finished with a raspberry emoji. I knew it was Rio. It had to be.

❦

That was all before Mia. And Danny Cash. And Nicky Dulgence and Gary Reed. Before life had become so exciting, I could hardly think straight.

That was before I'd started to worry about what on earth I was going to do at Danny Cash's training session. Me, 'Billy the Flid'. What was I going to bring to the beautiful game? I thought about what Mia had done earlier and my mind started racing. They thought she was so cool. I could do all that stuff and more. I could be cool as well. If I could just pluck up the courage to show them…

3.

Fever Pitch

'So, what have we got in our packed lunches today then?' asked Mrs Welbeck, our Learning Support Assistant. She peered at us through her thick-rimmed glasses with her fixed half smile.

Mia looked at the floor all around her. 'I'm sorry, I thought there must be a three-year-old in here,' she said with a hostile glare.

I felt embarrassed so I said, 'I've got a Dairylea sandwich with no crusts and a strawberry yoghurt and a banana.'

It was my turn to get the Mia glare which was hardly fair. Mrs Welbeck is kind and anyway, she has to ask because my cerebral palsy means that it's hard for me to eat certain foods. I might choke and she needs to make sure I'm safe. It's what she's paid for. She helps us both use the toilet afterwards too, at least, that's the idea. Actually, she just helps me.

Mia says, 'I'd sooner wet meself.' Sometimes she can be quite rude.

Mrs Welbeck was a dinner lady before she became an LSA. She was a good dinner lady.

'Do you think you can manage alright, love?' said Mrs Welbeck.

I nodded. She didn't dare ask Mia for fear of getting a mouthful. Dinner times have become awkward, truth be known.

When we'd finished and I'd used the toilet, Mrs Welbeck said, 'I'll see you both later for PE.'

She supports us for PE too. We had geography first.

'Oh goody,' said Mia, when Mrs Welbeck was probably still within earshot.

'Why are you being so nasty to her?' I said. 'She's only trying to help. It's her job.'

'Treating me like a toddler does *not* help me,' said Mia. 'I don't know how you endure it.'

'We need extra support, Mia. You know we do,' I said.

'Billy, I know this is a personal question and if you say "yes" then I'll respect that and if you say "mind your own business" I'll respect that too, but do you really, seriously need help using the toilet? What do you do at home, ask your mum?'

I was not enjoying this conversation. Lots of people need assistance with personal hygiene, there's no shame in it. I used to be one of them, but now I'm not.

'No, I can manage … thank you very much,' I said.

'Then why why WHY do you need Mrs Bloomin' Welbeck to hold your hand, or whatever on earth she does hold, when you're in school?'

I felt myself going red. Mrs Welbeck had been my LSA in primary school and came up to secondary with me. In those days, she used to be with me all of the time, not just for PE and dinners. She's nice. A little earnest, but ... nice.

'Because she always has done,' I said, blushing. 'I don't want to be rude.'

'Oh my God,' said Mia. 'That's not a *reason*. Do you think she enjoys it? You don't have to be rude, Billy. Just say, "I can manage now, thank you ever so much, Mrs Welbeck." Or you could just tell her to bog off.'

Mia seems to have an opinion on everything and even when she's wrong, she says it in such a way that you can't argue. At least *I* can't.

'When you're ready, thank you,' said Mr Balotelli. We'd lost the first five minutes of geography, as usual, to late arrivals, chairs and tables scraping, Rio and his mates messing about at the back, people like me and Mia chatting.

Our tutor room now looked like a shrine to Earl's Court FC. We'd gone nuts; everyone had joined in, even kids who supported other teams. There was a giant blue and yellow flag on the back wall with the words **JUST LIKE WATCHING BRAZIL** printed on it; the letters **E C F** and **C** had been cut out, painted blue and yellow, and stuck on the windows so that they could be read from outside; photos of Earl's Court players and England players adorned the room, especially Nicky Dulgence, Gary Reed and, of course, Danny Cash; seventeen Earl's Court scarves were draped over anything that didn't move but school rules said that we weren't allowed to wear them, or replica shirts, so there were nine of those pinned to the walls.

Mr Balotelli is tall but he doesn't scare anyone. He stoops and looks constantly ready to apologise.

He said, 'OK. This should be a nice easy lesson for me as *you* are going to do all the work. There are thirteen non-British players in the Earl's Court first team squad; their names and nationalities are on the whiteboard. I want you to work in your groups and decide among yourselves how you are going to make a presentation to the class, based on the country of origin of at least one of those players. This presentation will be at the end of the lesson and will last five minutes. It should include the salient geographical features of that country including population, population density, demographic make-up, terrain, GDP etc. I want you to show how these features relate to each other. The presentation can take any form you choose – before you ask, yes Tyreece, including rap and no Tyreece, not including foul and abusive language. You have half an hour and you can use audio-visual aids if you wish…'

And so on. Brilliant. This was how school was now that the visit from the Earl's Court players was imminent. Most of the teachers jumped on the bandwagon. In maths, Mr Lawrenson had us working out the percentage of various clubs' income that was spent on players' wages and how closely that correlated with success on the pitch. In science, Mr Moore asked us to work out the force imparted when kicking a ball (not much in my case) and the effect of playing football on your breathing and heart rate. We were designing and making scale models of a new stadium using materials of our own choice for Mrs Claridge in DT and writing match reports for different audiences for Mr Bowles in English. In philosophy and RE, Ms Do Nascimento had us discussing 'Football as the New Religion: Can Danny Cash Lead us to the Promised Land?' I'm not sure if Ms Do Nascimento takes her job entirely seriously.

Shanika was our team leader for the geography

presentation. We chose Nigeria: ECFC left-back Tunje Babatunde's home and also Shanika's dad's.

Shanika is a good team leader. She tries to include everyone but, as usual, I was too shy to speak out. That's until she said, 'OK, we've covered geography, population, the economy … I think that's enough unless someone has a different idea.'

And I said, 'How about sport?'

I was so nervous it came out sounding like I was being strangled, but I said it.

'What was that, Billy? I didn't hear.'

'What about sport? Nigeria is a great football nation.'

Hisham started to mock me but Shanika just talked over him.

'Yes, brilliant,' said Shanika. 'But I don't know anything about football…'

'I do,' I said, but Hisham said the same words at the same time and everyone looked at him.

'Tell us about Nigerian football, Hisham,' said Shanika.

Hisham looked panicked. 'Well, um, they wear green and … they…'

Hisham trailed off and looked embarrassed. I was feeling bolder and said, 'Nigeria won the African Cup of Nations in 1980, 1994 and 2013.'

'Really?' said Shanika. 'That's brilliant. Anything else?'

My voice was getting stronger. 'They were once ranked fifth in the world by FIFA.'

'How do you know this stuff?'

Hisham glared at me with real hatred, but he's not brave when Rio's not around.

'I like football. I read up about it online and watch loads of old matches.'

'Billy, you're a star,' said Shanika.

I sing like Scooby Doo and public speaking is definitely *not* my strong point (now, public squeaking – none better) so Shanika decided we would be inclusive and present Nigeria through the medium of mime. My job was to hold up large information cards while the other seven kids silently acted that information out. We had some really cool music playing while we did it, which Shanika said was Yoruba and I wasn't going to argue.

Here's how it went. I rolled by holding up a – slightly wobbly – card saying: NIGERIA ARE THREE TIMES WINNERS OF THE AFRICAN CUP OF NATIONS AND WERE ONCE RANKED FIFTH IN THE WORLD while the rest of the group pretended to play football. Hisham got a sly kick into Tomasz's shin and he didn't look happy but I quickly held up the next card. NIGERIA'S CAPITAL IS ABUJA BUT THE BIGGEST CITY IS LAGOS WHICH HAS AN EXTREMELY DENSE POPULATION OF OVER 21 MILLION PEOPLE while the others demonstrated this by huddling really close together, shoving and elbowing each other. I held up a card proclaiming: NIGERIA IS HALF MUSLIM AND HALF CHRISTIAN while four kids faced East, pretending to pray while the other three mimed being crucified. I had to spread my arms and pretend to be nailed to the cross too, to get the proportions right.

It was good. We got more laughs than any of the other groups although, to be fair, we weren't really going for comedy. I was pleased to see that Adedoja, Yakubu and Sakinah seemed to be taking it far more seriously.

It was a real shame that we had to cut the presentation short. I showed a card saying: NIGERIA'S BIGGEST CURRENT PROBLEM IS ETHNIC VIOLENCE IN THE OIL PRODUCING NIGER DELTA REGION but (Horrible) Hisham, (Terrible) Tyrell, (Jackass) Jack and (Tiresome) Tomasz got more than a little carried away with their mime and Mr Balotelli got a couple of nasty kicks when he had to separate them.

Still, once Mr B. had got those four into different corners of the room and called Mrs Footman, the school nurse, to sort out Hisham's head wound, he did say, 'Thank you, Blue Group. That was … quite extraordinary.'

Result. And it felt so good being part of a team and actually contributing some good stuff, even if we did all have to stay back and clear up the blood and broken furniture.

Everyone was getting more and more excited. The whole tutor group was reaching fever pitch. Two days to wait until DANNY CASH!

4.

Experience

'If I had the wings of a sparrow,' sang Rio. 'If I had the wings of a crow, I'd fly over Chelsea tomorrow, and...'

'That's quite enough, Rio. We do *not* need to hear the rest of that song,' said Mr Marsh, our PE teacher.

'How come you know it, sir? Do you sing it an' all?'

'You can start with twenty press-ups, Rio, and it will be thirty the next time you are rude, cheeky or disruptive in my class. Forty for the following time, then fifty. You get my drift? By the end of this year, you'll be looking like the Incredible Hulk unless you change your ways pretty damn sharpish. Get down on the floor NOW. One, two, three...'

Rio is definitely the coolest kid in the class but most of us are scared of him too. Sometimes he just hits other kids, for no reason at all. He gets Liam or Hisham to video it on their mobiles. They think it's a laugh. Mr Marsh isn't scared of Rio. I don't think Mr Marsh is scared of anybody. Mr Marsh is what my mum would call 'an aggressive shorts wearer'. He wears the shortest, tightest shorts and he wears them all of the time. Even when there's snow on the ground and icicles on your nose, Mr Marsh is thrusting his muscular thighs and his manly, scarred knees in our faces. Metaphorically that is – there I go again.

Normally no one messes around in PE but then normally, we haven't got three top footballers coming into our school the next day. We were all getting way too excited.

'We need,' said Mr Marsh, 'to improve our ball skills by about six hundred per cent if we are not to look like a bunch of muppets tomorrow. When I say, "six hundred", I mean, of course, "six thousand". When I say "we", I mean, of course, "you". As you might or might not know, I was on the books at Brentford Football Club with an illustrious career ahead of me, when cruciate ligament damage plucked me from the jaws of fame and fortune and deposited me in the talent-free zone that is Willesden Junction Community School, heaven help me.'

I don't think Mr Marsh is a happy man. In fact, I think he is bitter. He takes it out on the kids in his classes. Except me. He doesn't know what to do with me.

'When Danny Cash, or Gary Reed, or Nicky Dulgence ask you to pass, head or control the ball tomorrow, it would be a treat for all of us if you could at least remain upright while doing so. Let's at least *try* not to look like a special school. No offence, Billy and Mia.'

Me and Mia looked at each other and each raised an eyebrow. Just a tiny little bit, so that no one else could see. It's so good when you start to get an understanding with someone.

When I was six, it felt good when my mum told me I was 'special'. Those days are long gone. Now I know that 'special' means social outcast. It means living in fear of being side-lined, left on the bench. Do you fancy my kind of 'special'? Thought not.

'…nineteen, twenty.' Rio finished his press-ups and sprang to his feet without using his hands. There was a little gasp and some clapping. His body works so well and I hate him for it, and I hate myself for hating him for it. If that makes any sense.

One time, I did a bad thing. Maybe more than one time. I'm not proud of it but I was only a kid. It was in primary school, when me and Rio were mates. Rio's parents were breaking up and they were fighting all the time and it was seriously nasty. Rio was taking it badly and his behaviour became terrible. He messed around in class, cheeked our teacher and was constantly looking for a fight. He was just looking for excuses to hit people. I gave him some excuses. I'd say that someone had been horrible to me when they hadn't. Things like, 'Rio, Jaden called me a spaz.' And that would be it: Jaden on the floor with a bloody nose.

It felt good because it was power. I've never had any power. I know it was bad really but it gave me a chance to get back at some mean people and it's not like I was actually doing the punching. It was more like a video game really; I just had to press the right buttons. Sometimes I wondered if Rio ever found out what I was doing.

Rio ran his hand over his product-soaked hair. He wasn't even breathing heavily.

'Thank you, Rio. Right,' said Mr Marsh, 'in your groups. There are four activities. We will all do each one of them in a rota. Number one: Piggy in the Middle – pass the ball amongst yourselves while keeping it away from the "piggy". The hands may not be used. If the piggy touches the ball at all then they are no longer in the middle, the half-wit that passed it is. Number two: controlling the ball with one touch, passing with the second, moving at all times. Make sure everyone is included, not just your bestest mates. Number three: Keepy Uppy in pairs or threes if necessary. The pair or three with the highest number of touches without the ball hitting the ground will receive the coveted prize of not being shouted at by me. Number four: dribbling the ball around each and every one of the cones and then back again, like so…'

Mr Marsh demonstrated. His thigh muscles bulged intimidatingly as he rounded each cone. He's good. Maybe he was telling the truth about being with Brentford FC.

'When you have finished or, perhaps I should say, *if* you manage to finish, you give the ball to your teammate who will do the same. Billy and Mia, you will practise throwing and catching skills with Mrs Welbeck. You all know what you are doing. GO.'

I said that Mr Marsh doesn't know what to do with me, which is true but he thinks he does. Before Mia came, he would get me throwing and catching a ball with Mrs Welbeck. Before I got to secondary, I spent most of my PEs in primary school throwing and catching a ball with Mrs Welbeck. Now that Mia is here, I spend PE throwing and catching a ball with Mrs Welbeck and Mia. I'm pretty good at throwing and catching. Pretty sick of it too. Here was a perfect opportunity for me and Mia to practise some skills and actually make an impression on the footballers tomorrow and Mr Marsh just wanted to get us out of the way.

The other groups were making lots of noise but it was a good noise, the noise that the best teachers look for. It was the sound of enthusiasm. Everyone wanted to do well for the visit of Danny Cash and the others. No one wanted to look foolish. Some of the boys reckoned they might get signed up by Earl's Court if they could really impress. Not this boy. Everybody was trying their best and Mr Marsh was hardly shouting at all. The best pair at Keepy Uppy were Tyreece and Rio. Obviously.

Mia's face was a picture as she threw the ball to me. Not a very nice picture. It was a picture of boredom and barely suppressed anger. I caught the ball and threw it back.

'To me, Mia,' said Mrs Welbeck.

Mia slowly turned her head and fixed her with a glare but threw the ball to, or should I say, *at* me. I wasn't expecting it so I spilled the catch. Mrs Welbeck picked the ball up.

'That wasn't terribly helpful, Mia,' she said.

'I'm sorry, miss,' said Mia, not sounding sorry at all, 'but this is *boring*. It's boring now, it was boring last week and it will be even more boring next week. Please, please, *please* can we do something else?'

I looked down at the floor.

'Well, if you're *that* bored, you can always ask Mr Marsh if you like,' said Mrs Welbeck. She didn't think Mia would have the guts. She really doesn't get Mia.

'Mr Marsh, sir,' shouted Mia. He looked over. 'This is really boring and it's all we ever do. Can we do something different please?'

Mr Marsh stared at Mia. 'OK. Groups change. Move on to your next activity. Mia and Billy, I'd like you to develop your skills and *bounce* the ball to each other. I hope that's not *too* boring for you, Mia. Let's go everybody.'

I hardly dared look at Mia. Mrs Welbeck said, 'Come on, you two. Let's make the best of this.'

I bounced the ball to Mia who caught it and threw it, deliberately, at the wheels of my chair. It ricocheted into the Piggy in the Middle group, spoiling what they were doing.

'Oops,' said Mia.

Mr Marsh side-footed the ball gently back to Mrs Welbeck. She picked it up and bounced it back to Mia, who did the same thing again. This time, the ball bounced into Eboni, who was trying to do Keepy Uppies with Shannon.

'Oops,' said Mia.

'Aaand, STOP,' said Mr Marsh. He glared hard at Mia but said nothing.

'Are you going to make me do press-ups, *sir*?' she asked. She was glaring right back at him.

'No, Mia. I'm going to give you a detention. If

you want to waste our time, then we're going to waste yours. This lesson is over for you. Go and get changed please. Mrs Welbeck, could you accompany Mia?'

Mia spun her wheelchair around and began heading to the girls' changing room. It was a flounce on wheels.

'What do you think, Billy?' said Mr Marsh. 'Do my PE lessons bore *you* as well?'

Pretty much my worst nightmare. The whole class was staring at me, waiting for my reply. Some of the boys were grinning … no, leering. Even Mia stopped and turned to look. There was no escaping it. I had to speak. My mind was racing at a thousand miles an hour, trying out responses in my head: responses like 'no sir', or 'of course not sir, I like PE', or even just a headshake – that would do it.

Do you know what actually came out of my mouth? This: 'Mia's right, sir. You always get me and her throwing and catching. It's … not very interesting. We want to do something different.'

Where did *that* come from?

Mia smiled at me before carrying on into the girls' changing room with Mrs Welbeck. It was the first time she had ever smiled at me. I felt a surge of *something* in my stomach that I'd never felt before. It was good.

This wasn't. Mr Marsh said nothing for a bit. He was thinking about impersonating my squeaky voice, I could tell he was.

But he didn't. He said, 'Do you now? Do you really? OK, Billy, this should be a new and wonderful experience for you. You can join the Red Group doing Piggy in the Middle. Guess what? *You* are the Piggy until the end of the session.'

Red Group were Orla, Haadiya, (Loathsome) Luca, Jordan, Adedoja, (Horrible) Hisham and, of course, (The Evil) Rio.

'Here, Piggy Piggy,' said Rio, setting the tone as I rolled up.

They made a circle around me and started passing the ball between themselves.

'It's Billy the Pig,' said Luca.

I couldn't even get near it.

'Maybe you'll be on Spaz of the Day, tonight,' said Jordan and he started singing the *Match of the Day* music. OK, that means he needs a nickname too – Jelly-Face Jordan.

Mr Marsh could hear what was happening but he did nothing to stop it.

'We wan a duh somfin diffunt…' said Hisham, bouncing the ball off the right wheel of my chair, back to himself.

The ball and the taunts always seemed to be behind me.

'Hey, it's squeals on wheels,' said Orla. Now 'Orrible Orla.

I managed not to cry, just. The frustration and the taunting went on and on. Of course, I wanted to practise my skills but Mr Marsh just wanted to humiliate me. Red Group were happy to help. It seemed like forever until Mr Marsh finally blew his whistle.

'That's it everybody. Thank you for your efforts today. If you show that much application tomorrow, Messrs Cash, Reed and Dulgence will be impressed. Balls in the bag please, cones in the cupboard, then get changed. I want you dressed, ready and lined up by half past two, not a second later. Billy, I do hope you enjoyed your experience. Perhaps on Wednesday, you could show off your skills to Danny Cash. Maybe Earl's Court will sign you up.'

Some kids sniggered and Mr Marsh walked away with an ugly smile on his face.

'Yeah spaz-bag, you could teach him how to dribble,' said Orla.

'You could nutmeg him.'

'You could show him your overhead kick…'

'…or how to jump for a header.'

Were they right? Standing up to Mr Marsh made

me braver. Made me think maybe, just maybe, I could do something to impress. Impress everyone, not just the footballers. Show them what I *can* do. Not just what I can't.

Mrs Welbeck helped me get changed, although I really don't need help anymore. I thought about how I could tell her. I think my physio must really be working. It takes me a while, but I can do it myself now. Though I wonder if that would leave me vulnerable to bullying in the changing room.

Mia was waiting for me outside the gym.

'Thanks Billy, and well done for standing up to Mr Marsh; it's the only thing to do with bullies. I'm sorry I called you a spaz the other day. I was wrong.'

Mia smiled at me again and just like that, everything was alright.

There was a lot to tell Nettle.

5.

The Squoken Word

*in 17 hours and 3 minutes time I will be playing football
with Nicky Dulgence, Gary Reed and Danny Cash*

I posted to my online friends. It felt amazing.

I'm a member of several (five) social networking sites and online forums. It's cool because in some of them (three) I've never mentioned my condition and in some of them (you've got it – two) I have, so I get the best of both worlds. I used to have different names in all of them: billythekid7, billyt, billywhiz and earl billy but now I've got the same name in all of them. I changed it. Now I'm just Raz Beri.

'I know, Nettle,' I said to the one-eyed hairball on my lap. 'I hate boasters too, but sometimes you just have to tell it like it is.'

I played an old-school Pac-Man game on my laptop while I waited for the replies to start flooding in but I had barely started when I heard the triple bleep that told me a text had dropped into my mobile. I don't get a lot of texts, except for nasty ones, but I knew who it might be and let me tell you, this was a VERY EXCITING DEVELOPMENT. After that scary PE lesson, Mia and I had exchanged mobile numbers. I know. How awesome is that?

Before I tell you about Mia's text, there are two things you need to know about me and my mobile: one totally cool and one totally sad. The totally cool thing is that I've got a special mobile that recognises my voice and does what I tell it to, even converting my spoken words into texts. No need for thumb ache. I've learned to check really carefully though as it sometimes makes mistakes because my voice isn't always so clear.

Once my mum was shopping at the supermarket and I went to the fridge and finished off the ice cream. There was only a couple of spoonfuls left. I sent her a text saying:

don't forget ice cream

But my phone converted my words to:

don't forget I scream

She texted back saying:

> *not heard you scream since you were*
> *little babes but I definitely wont forget!*

Which I didn't think was very funny. And then she brought the wrong ice cream back. She brought vanilla which is so boring. She said she was laughing too hard to notice.

The totally sad thing is that I have never made or received a phone call on my mobile phone. That's how popular I am and that's how self-conscious I am about my voice.

Here's a thought: if you speak and I squeak, then when you spoke, I squoke, and when you have spoken, I must have squoken. Well, the squoken word text facility is a lifesaver for people like me.

Mia's text read:

> *ta for sticking up for me today. You see, you can*
> *stand up like a man – who knows what else*
> *you can do? X*

OK, firstly: she didn't use text-speak – YEAH! Secondly: that was the first text I'd ever had with a kiss at the end – YEAH! Thirdly: she seemed genuinely impressed with me – YEAH! Fourthly: wow! Fifthly: WOW! Sixthly: WOW WOW WOW!!! I felt like squawking it from the rooftops.

I completely forgot about my online conversation. I love my virtual friends but real ones are ten times better.

'Nettle. What on earth do I text back?'

I even thought about asking my mum what to do but she'd gone out. She'd recently started going out and leaving me alone in the evenings a lot. It's a bit scary but, as she says, I'm not a little boy anymore. She was dressed up. She had make-up on. She'd done something ridiculous with her hair. She said, 'You got my mobile number, which you can use in emergencies, not that there're gonna be any. Make sure you're in bed by ten, you got school tomorrow – I'm trusting you here, Billy. Don't wait for me to get back; I got a date. See ya tomorrow, babes.'

I don't like her in make-up.

I said to Nettle, 'I'm just gonna play it cool. Can I do cool?'

She wasn't listening. She was barking and bouncing her solitary front paw down on my keyboard:

ma me

'Nettle, you are *so* not helping.'

Nettle kept on barking. Or rather, yapping. Or rather, yipping.

'Nettle, will you SHUT UP.' She looked hurt and stopped her racket. I picked up my mobile phone.

'OK. **Billy's phone – REPLY**,' I said. The screen changed, ready to write.

'*No probs,*' I dictated, '*anything to help. Are you excited about tomorrow?* **Billy's phone – SEND**.' No kiss. I forgot the kiss. How on earth do you dictate a kiss to a machine?

My mobile wrote the message out perfectly and sent it – yes! Too perfect really. Only old people use perfect spelling and correct punctuation but I was sure Mia would understand. Nettle eyed me sullenly and pawed at the keyboard.

'You're obsessed with my laptop, Nettle. What's got into you?'

Nettle looked at me expectantly and my mobile triple bleeped to tell me I had another text. Mia!

well, i'm not excited by text table tennis.
Can you give me a call – ive got no credit. X

That feeling I had when I had to speak up in front of Mr Marsh? Same feeling now. Icy fingers worming their way through my intestines, giving them a little squeeze here, a tiny tug there. Mia's got this knack of taking me to places that I don't want to go. Or maybe places that I do want to go to but never knew it. Or realised that I could.

'Everyone else makes phone calls, Net…'

Everyone else has a voice that doesn't sound like it needs pumping up and oiling.

But Billy Turpin, superstar, yours is the one that Mia has just said she wants to hear.

Wow, there was a time when I could only hear fearful voices in my head but it seems that I've got some brave ones too. *And* they're muscling their way to the front.

'**Billy's phone – CALL MIA.**' There, done it. I heard the dialling tone for the first time. The icy fingers inside grabbed a good handful and squeezed.

'Hey you,' said Mia.

Omigod. This is where you talk, Billy. 'Hiya, you alright?'

'Yeah,' said Mia. She can hear me! She can understand me! 'Sorry about getting you to call but I'm nearly out of credit and exchanging texts all evening does my head in anyway. What you up to?'

'Not a lot,' I said. 'My mum's out on a date so I'm just chilling with my dog.'

'Uh huh. No Dad then. I got a dad but I ain't got a mum. At least, not one that could be bothered to hang around,' said Mia, like she was talking about the weather.

'Does your dad look after you then?'

'*I* look after me, Billy, and I look after my dad too. Someone's got to wake him up, take the whisky glass out of his hand and send him off to bed.'

'Oh,' I said. I didn't know what else to say.

'Don't sound so shocked, Billy,' said Mia. 'My dad's great and he brought me up all by himself when I was little, but it can't be easy having a famous brother who earns three hundred thousand pounds a week for kicking a piece of leather around.'

'Your Uncle Danny.'

'Yeah,' said Mia. 'My Uncle Danny. Time was, my dad was supposed to be the next big star, the new Wayne Rooney. Danny Cash was just Owen Cash's little brother.'

'So, what happened?' I so wasn't expecting this conversation.

'*I* happened, Billy. Rising star, Owen Cash's girlfriend squeezed out a baby raspberry ripple, took one look and ran off into the deep blue yonder. My dad, at least, faced up to his responsibility but whisky mixes better with Coke than with football. The likes of you and me, Billy, are not what a new parent wants to see.'

My mind was racing. 'I wonder if that's why my dad went away.'

'Wow, you're quick, Billy.'

This was heavy stuff but I wasn't scared of talking to Mia on the phone. It felt really good.

'Maybe your mum went off with my dad,' I said but Mia didn't laugh. I changed the subject to something I'd been trying to figure out.

'Listen,' I said. 'Danny Cash is white…'

'Yehsssss…'

'So, your dad must be white…'

'Well, not necessarily, but yehssss…'

'And you're … not…'

'Noooo…'

'So … your mum…'

'Yehssss?'

I was seriously wishing I hadn't started this.

'…must be Black.'

'Well,' said Mia. 'We were pretty close for about nine months, and I haven't seen her since, but yes, she was. And presumably still is. You're on fire, mate. You should be on *Mastermind*.'

My mum says sarcasm is the lowest form of humour. I changed the subject again.

'What's Danny Cash like then, I mean, your Uncle Danny?' I said.

'We don't see a lot of him really,' said Mia. 'Just Christmas and family stuff. He's too busy playing football all over the world and enjoying his money. And before you ask, no, we don't see a penny of it. I'm lucky if Dad can afford oil for my wheelchair.'

'I wasn't going to ask. I thought you said your Uncle Danny would do anything for you?'

'People say a lot of things, Billy. Danny Cash is everyone's hero; I know he's yours. Look, that's fine but really, he's just an ordinary bloke. Not horrible, not lovely. He just happens to be rich and famous. People believe what they want to about him, I suppose.'

'I think he's amazing,' I said. It sounded so lame.

'And I *know* he's not but he *is* good at playing football and tomorrow should be fun,' said Mia. Her words were nearly drowned out by another demented flurry of yipping by Nettle.

'Either that's your dog or you've got even more issues with your voice than I realised,' said Mia.

'Will you just SHUT IT. Bad girl,' I said.

'Hey!' said Mia.

'No, not you,' I said. 'Sorry Mia.' Although I've got to say, sometimes her sense of humour just isn't funny.

I paused and looked at the screen.

'Omigod,' I said.

'What? What's up?' said Mia.

'She's done it again,' I said. 'She jumps up on my keyboard and keeps writing the same thing…'

'Your dog? Yeah right. What does she write?'

'"ma me"', I said. 'Twice now, "ma me".'

'Mummy,' said Mia, laughing. 'She thinks you're her mummy.'

'Mia, she's a dog. She can't spell.'

'Yeah, and raspberries can't stand up to bullying teachers,' said Mia. 'Ask her your name, go on.'

'Don't be daft, she's a dog…'

'Billy, just do it.'

'Oh, for heaven's sake. OK, Nettle, what's my name?'

Nettle sneezed into my lap.

'Lovely. Nettle, what's my name?'

Nettle looked at me and barked.

I heard Mia laugh down the line. 'Congratulations, Mummy. You have a beautiful, hairy little girl.'

Like I said about Mia's sense of humour…

'Listen, Billy,' said Mia. Her tone of voice was suddenly completely different. Serious.

'What is it?'

'Billy, can you keep a secret? I mean a *real* secret. It's a huge one and I've been sitting on it forever but it feels like it's trying to get out by itself now. Billy, you're the person I've got to tell and you *will* understand why but I really can't do it on the phone.'

'Omigod. What is it?' I said.

'I'll tell you tomorrow, Billy. It's about my Uncle Danny.'

6.

Bad Stuff

D-Day. Danny-Day. When I woke up, I went for a wee, then looked at the replies I had received to my post last night. Loads, from the simple:

WOW! How come?

…to the brilliant, like this from my old online friend, Irenka:

lucky you, Raz. I know you love football, have you ever tried wheelchair football?

I hadn't but, blimey, what an amazing idea! So much stuff in my head, I thought it might explode.

School was crazy, right from the start. Mr Balotelli couldn't keep us quiet; he couldn't keep any sort of order while he tried to do the register. We were just too excited. 'Like herding cats,' my nan would have said.

I'd arrived into class, hoping to talk to Mia but she was surrounded by a gaggle of her mates and there was no way I could get to her, so I sat by myself and pretended to be sorting things out in my bag while Shannon, Shanika, Jaz, Precious and Eboni gossiped and giggled with *my* new best friend.

'Junaid?' said Mr Balotelli.

'Here, sir.'

'Rosella?'

'Yes, sir.'

'Rio?'

'Yeah.'

'Sir?' said Mr Balotelli.

'No need to call me sir, sir. Rio will do.'

Any kids that were listening, laughed.

'You're too kind, Rio. Jordan?'

No reply.

'Jordan?'

No reply.

'Jordan Downer, are you here?' said Mr Balotelli, looking straight at him.

'No, sir, I'm not very well today. I had to stay at home,' said Jordan, grinning. He's one of Rio's cronies so he can get away with that kind of thing.

'If only, Jordan, if only,' said Mr Balotelli, but kids were laughing too much to hear him.

There was no need to do the register really. Everyone was in. No one was going to miss the visit of Danny Cash and the others.

'Haadiya?'

'Yes, sir.'

'Precious?'

'Here, sir.'

'Billy?'

'Here, sir,' I said and everyone fell about laughing. Just for a change. Seriously, my voice seems to be getting squeakier. My mum says it's my age. I dread the morning and afternoon registers and when I'm nervous it just gets worse. Squeakage.

'Settle down, thank you,' said Mr Balotelli, but no one did.

'Sakinah?'

'Yes, sir.'

'Tomasz?' said Mr Balotelli.

But before Tomasz could answer, Rio said, 'Sir, you didn't ought to swear, sir. It teaches us bad habits.'

'What are you talking about, Rio? I didn't swear.'

'Yeah you did, sir. You said "Dumb-Ass".'

That was it. The class was gone. Everyone was laughing, even me. Even Tomasz. We were all so wound up by the footballers' visit that any little thing would set us off. Tyrell high-fived Rio. Liam started shouting randomly; he gets excited by noise.

'*Tom*-asz, I said *Tomasz*,' said Mr B above the commotion. He was going a dodgy colour.

'He said it again!' said Rio. 'Sir, don't call him that, it ain't fair. Just cos he's Polish and that … and a bit of a dumb-ass.'

'That's enough,' said Mr Balotelli. 'That's enough.'

But no one was listening. No one could hear above the laughter and the shouting.

That's when the door opened.

'Is everything alright, Mr Balotelli?' said Mr Marsh as he walked in. We were all quiet straight away. 'I heard a lot of noise.'

'Yes, thank you, Mr Marsh,' said Mr Balotelli. 'Some of the students are a little over-excited by the prospect of our famous visitors today.'

'And Mr Balotelli kept swearing at Tomasz, sir,' said Rio, grinning, but this time nobody laughed.

Mr Marsh walked over to Rio. He paused and said, 'It would be a terrible shame if anyone had to miss out on meeting Messrs Cash, Dulgence and Reed this afternoon but I'm sure you could find plenty of geography for them to catch up on, Mr Balotelli, if anyone becomes … too excited. Am I right?'

'You're absolutely right, Mr Marsh,' said Mr Balotelli. 'There's no shortage of work to do.'

'Well, if any student needs to come and explain to me why they will be missing our special PE this afternoon, you know where to send them, don't you, Mr Balotelli?'

'Indeed. Thank you, Mr Marsh,' said Mr B.

And that was that. Rio squashed, discipline regained and Mr Balotelli humiliated. It was turning into a very good day for Mr Marsh. For now.

'Orla?'

'Here, sir.'

'Yakubu?'

'Yes, sir.'

Mr Marsh turned on his heel with a flourish and walked out of the class. Nobody messed Mr Balotelli around anymore, in fact, all of the teachers had the easiest job keeping control after that. They just had to mention the possibility of missing 'the visit'.

I tried all morning to speak to Mia and find out about that secret, but I just couldn't get to her. Our chairs take up too much space to sit together in class and at break time Mia, Precious and Eboni were involved in a terrifying slanging match with Adedoja, Shanika and Akina. I wasn't going *near* that one and no one else was either.

When we'd nearly finished our dinner, Mia turned her back on Mrs Welbeck and said, 'You know I've got that detention after this don't you? I'll only have ten minutes before "the visit" so I'll meet you down the side of the gym at ten-to and I'll tell you about *that thing*. It won't take long.'

That thing. The secret. After dinner, I drifted aimlessly around the playground, pretending to be doing stuff with all my non-existent friends until it was nearly time.

The gym is as far away from the main school as you can get before you hit the path that goes into the woods down the side of the football pitches. At twelve-minutes-to, I was thinking about Mia and her secret as I approached our meeting spot. I heard one, then two people behind me blow raspberries, then snigger. I didn't look back. I could guess.

Rio's voice said, 'What you doing, spastic? Where's your minder, the lovely Mia?'

'Not all by yourself, are you?' said Hisham. 'No one to look after you? Bad move, mongo.'

'You remember when you used to get *me* to fight your battles for you, mong?' said Rio. 'Do you? Took me for a muppet, didn't ya? She'll get wise soon enough.'

Oh God, 'Rio, I'm…'

'Don't bother, bruv. Save your breath.'

'Yeah,' said Hisham. 'Save it for Danny Cash. You gotta show off your skills, spacker.'

'What you gonna do, spaz?' said Rio. 'I know, you can show him how fast you can go. Let's practise.'

This felt serious. Rio moved up behind me, grabbed the handles of my wheelchair and started pushing me violently.

I remembered Mia and I said, 'Let go! Let go of my wheelchair,' but my voice is so weak, I don't think they even heard it.

Hisham and Rio were whooping and taking turns to push me into the woods where the path gets rough and only bad stuff happens. To have my safety in Rio's hands was terrifying. I stopped my futile squawking and concentrated on staying in my chair, white knuckles gripping the hand rests.

'That's a sharp bend coming up, spaz,' shouted Rio. 'Reckon we can do it?'

I didn't. Wheelchairs aren't designed to take bends at speed and I was really moving now. We hit the apex (another word I learned at school) and I used my arm strength to throw myself sideways out of the chair to take charge of the fall and miss a tree. I tumbled into the undergrowth, my wheelchair on its side behind me with one wheel slowly spinning.

Nobody had seen. Rio and Hisham had to cling to each other, they were laughing so hard. I lay still, face down. Smelling the damp of the leaf mould, wondering what was coming next.

Rio disentangled himself from his mate and looked at his mobile. He took a photo of me and said, 'We gotta go, Hish. We got an appointment with some England football players. Shame you're gonna miss it, mong. We'll try and get you an autograph.'

Hisham laughed. Rio stopped laughing, stepped forward and put his boot on the back of my head.

'You thought you'd get special treatment, didn't you? Well, you just got it and if you say a dicky bird about this, spaz, you are dead meat. Ya get me?'

He pressed my face further into the dirt, then picked up my wheelchair, jumped in and said, 'I have an urgent appointment Mr Nazir and I wish to take my carriage. Let's hit the road.'

Hisham started pushing Rio back up the path but it's really hard to push a wheelchair uphill on rough ground so after about fifteen metres, they gave up and walked.

'See ya, mongo. Have fun.'

I waited until they were out of sight, and then waited a little bit more. Hisham and Rio must have walked right past Mia, waiting by the gym to tell me her secret. Wondering why I hadn't turned up. Cursing me to hell.

I had a bump growing already on my head and scratches on my face and hands. I touched my face to check for blood. There was some, not too much. I hauled myself up onto my elbows and started to claw my way out of the undergrowth. It was painfully slow. First, I scratched my hand on some brambles, then I stung my forearm on a nettle. It wasn't so bad, but that was when the tears started anyway. It felt like I'd been waiting all my life for this chance and there I was, lying in the dirt, a thousand miles away from my idols.

Mr Balotelli would be introducing Gary Reed, Nicky Dulgence and Danny Cash to the class right now.

7.

On Telly, YEAH!

My upper body is quite strong, for a skinny thirteen-year-old with CP anyway. Often wheelchair users can pile the weight on but my mum has always been really careful with my diet and I do exercises every day. Well, almost. My new physio, Petra, insists on it. She's even started me on an exercise routine for my legs. It's savage. She makes me wear shorts (trust me, not pretty). She makes me 'stand' and support myself on a frame, while she attaches these elastic ties to various parts of my legs. Then I have to push and pull against them in all different directions.

It makes me feel like a fly in a cobweb. I hate it, but do you know what? It might just be making a difference. I found that I could haul myself quite efficiently out of the undergrowth and I even managed to use my legs a bit to propel myself forward. I must have looked like some huge, helpless insect emerging from its cocoon but there was no one there to see.

My chair was about fifteen metres away and you'd be surprised how far that is when you're dragging yourself through the dirt. This would never have happened at primary school – Mrs Welbeck was with me all the time then. Instinctively, I looked around for her although I knew there was no point. She'd be drinking coffee in the staff room, telling everyone what a lovely lad I am and how rude Mia can be.

I wondered if anyone had noticed my absence. Maybe they would send out a search party. Who was I kidding? Not with three England players in the classroom. Who's going to be thinking about me? I felt like crying some more but instead I wiped the tears from my cheeks and thought to myself: what would Mia do? Well, first of all, she'd swear. Something bad. I swore, something bad. You are *so* not allowed to say that word at school but it felt good so I kept on going; I cursed Rio and Hisham in the loudest voice I could manage and vowed to get my own back. Somehow. That felt good too. Are you meant to feel good about revenge? I thought about this as I heaved myself along and decided that in this case it was OK and by that time, I found that I had nearly got to my wheelchair.

That's what Mia would do: Mia would get back by herself, no matter how hard it was, no matter how long it took. No matter what. She'd get back and she'd show them that she didn't care, that they couldn't hurt her.

So, I stopped crying. I doubled my efforts and I crawled and I slithered like something gross you might find under a stone. And I reached my wheelchair. I was bloodied, filthy and exhausted. I reckoned I could haul myself in, if I put the handbrake on. It took another five minutes; I was breathing heavily and my muscles hurt but I did it. Now for the hard part.

One of the first things you learn when you are disabled is how to be free in your head, even if your body imprisons you. My computer lets me talk to anyone, anywhere, lets me fight terrorists and aliens, lets me beat Barcelona single-handedly in the Champions League final. That's all great, and sometimes it's a lifesaver, but my mind? My mind lets me run and jump and dance and sing and fly if I want to. In my mind I can run marathons, climb mountains and dance the fandango – whatever *that* is. In my mind, the world listens to my voice. And doesn't laugh. Maybe even thinking these things, makes them just a tiny little bit more likely to happen.

Pushing your wheelchair up a slope, on rough ground, is hard. It's the hardest thing I've done. My mind was doing all that brilliant stuff while I did it. I found I could move a few centimetres at a time, first one side, then the next. Then, handbrake on and rest. And again. And again. Inching past the spots where Rio and Hisham's running feet had fallen; through the echoes of their whooping and laughter. Slowly slogging through leaves and mud, sticks and slugs. Across the tarmac playground where I could actually get some momentum going and my burning muscles found relief. They cater well for wheelchair-users in my school, unlike in most places: there are ramps for every step, lifts for every flight of steps and the external doors are all automated. I pushed myself up the ramp and through the doors of the main building.

My tutor group was in 6A. When I reached the door, I waited outside for a minute trying to get my breath back. I'd done it! Me! Billy Turpin. I could hear unusual voices from inside – not teacher accents but footballer ones. From Essex, from Liverpool and Newcastle.

There were less than ten minutes left. The door was slightly ajar so I rolled myself forward and let my footrest push it open.

The talking stopped. Inside I saw Danny Cash, Nicky Dulgence and Gary Reed (Oh-My-God) in their tracksuits and some man in a shiny suit who I didn't like the look of. They were all standing in front of the class. This would be the Question-and-Answer session we'd planned so carefully with Mr Balotelli. I saw Rio and Hisham looking at me apprehensively. I saw Mia mouthing, 'Where the hell have you been?' I saw two photographers with expensive-looking camera equipment. I saw a man with a hand-held TV camera and the woman from the local news programme who is way smaller than she looks on TV. I saw Mr Balotelli and the rest of the class, staring at me like I was from Planet Zaaarg. Maybe I am but I knew that I'd done it. By myself. No help from my mum, from Mia, from Mrs Welbeck. Just me. Rio and Hisham knew it too. It felt good.

They saw a sweat-soaked thirteen-year-old in a filthy wheelchair, in damp, muddy clothing with unidentifiable smears down his front. They heard a scratched and sweaty raspberry squeak, 'Sorry, sir. I fell out of my wheelchair down in the woods.' And they nearly all sniggered.

Mr Balotelli clearly hadn't noticed my absence and obviously no one had thought to tell him either.

Mr B looked flustered and said, 'For goodness sake, Billy. Are you alright?'

'Yes, sir.'

'Come and find a space, Billy. You know our visitors, of course…'

'Yeah,' I said. 'Hi Danny, hi Nicky, hi Gary.'

Danny Cash just ignored me. Nicky Dulgence nodded towards me without making eye-contact and Gary Reed said, 'Alright, Billy? I hope you didn't hurt yourself.'

Wow, wow, wow … Gary Reed is talking to me. I shook my head and went red.

'OK, we're getting a liiittle short of time here,' said the man in the shiny suit.

'Sorry, Mr Lustig-Prean,' said Mr Balotelli. 'What do we need to do now?'

Mia says that Mr Lustig-Prean is what's known as a PR man. He's on this planet to make sure that idiot celebrities don't say anything offensive or that might conceivably be of interest. He had a Rolex watch and a voice like vanilla ice cream.

'We'll do that interview for the local news, then get some photos taken before the training session,' said Mr Lustig-Prean. His face was even shinier than his suit and he sported a tiny diamond stud in his right ear.

The woman from the local news moved in towards Danny Cash with her microphone and her phoney smile. The cameraman positioned himself so that he could get the table with Eboni, Misbah, Tyrell and Umehabibah on it in the background. Nicky Dulgence and Gary Reed stationed themselves so that it looked like they were helping them with their work: they squatted between the kids, pointing at random things in their books and smiling encouragingly.

The thin woman from the local news asked some banal question and Danny Cash said, 'Obviously, we're in a very privileged position, playing the game we love for good reward, but we're not motivated by money. We just want to give something back to the community,' in his amazing Liverpool accent. I saw Mia roll her eyes in irritation at her Uncle Danny.

Mr Lustig-Prean clutched the sides of his face, theatrically. 'What am I thinking of? Minorities, minorities! We can't be seen to exclude our "differently-abled" supporters. Mr Balotelli, nobody told me that you had um, wheelchair-users in your class. Would it be possible to get one of them into the shot?'

'Of course,' said Mr Balotelli. 'Billy, do you think you could squeeze yourself in between Umehabibah and Tyrell?'

My heart was going like a train after my exertions as it was. Then Gary Reed talks to me, then they want me on telly behind Danny Cash! Oh … My … G—

'No, actually,' said Mr Lustig-Prean. 'I was thinking more…' and he turned to look at Mia, 'you, young lady, I don't know your name. Yes you, Black or minority ethnic, wheelchair-using … female … studenty person. Come and do some work with my boys and get yourself on TV tonight.'

Mr Lustig-Prean strutted behind Mia and began to wheel her across the classroom floor. I forgot to feel crushed, I was so scared of what Mia might say and I wasn't wrong.

Danny Cash is almost as famous for his swearing as he is for his football but what came out of Mia's mouth left even him looking stunned. I wish I could tell you what she told Mr Lustig-Prean to do, I really do. It was angry, funny, creative and utterly obscene, all at the same time. Casting my mind back to biology lessons, I'm *almost* certain that it's physically impossible too, even for a non-disabled person but I guess I'm not an expert on these matters.

Mr Lustig-Prean went very pale and let go of Mia's wheelchair. The lady from the local news turned to the cameraman and said, 'Please tell me you got that.'

'Good grief, Mr Balotelli,' said Lustig-Prean. 'How do you cope with your job?'

'Therapy, thumb-sucking and industrial quantities of Cabernet Sauvignon,' whispered Mr Balotelli, before saying, in the loud voice he uses when trying to be authoritative. 'Mia, we'll talk later about this.'

But I knew that was nonsense. He'd just try to

forget it and pretend it never happened. I think he's even more scared of Mia than he is of Rio.

'I do apologise, Mr Lustig-Prean, some of the students are a little over-excited.'

'We'll use the other one,' said Lustig-Prean. 'The sweaty one.' Then he muttered under his breath, 'Hopefully the civilised one.'

I didn't look very civilised given what had happened before my entrance, but after what Mia had just said, I guess I was the only option. Mr Lustig-Prean couldn't possibly miss out on playing the equality and diversity card correctly now, could he?

'Willy,' he said, looking at me. 'Come on, it's your moment of glory.'

Guess what, no one corrected him, regarding my actual name. I would've done it myself, if it didn't already feel like my heart was going to burst out of my chest.

I squeezed myself in between Tyrell and Umehabibah. The camera started rolling. The skinny lady from the local news asked the same stupid question.

Nicky Dulgence pointed at a blank page in my geography book, smiled and whispered, 'Blimey, this is a bunch of crap,' to Gary Reed as he did so.

Danny Cash said, 'Obviously, we're in a very

privileged position, playing the game we love for good reward, but we're not motivated by money. We just want to give something back to the community.'

Mr Lustig-Prean mouthed the words as Danny Cash said them.

I smiled my most grateful smile at Nicky Dulgence (NICKY DULGENCE!) as if he'd just taught me the secret of life.

'That was a thing of great beauty. Thank you, people,' said Mr Lustig-Prean. 'We'll have two minutes of photos for the newspapers, then move on to the playing field for the training session.'

I looked over Nicky Dulgence's shoulder at my tutor group. Most were looking envious, especially Rio. Mia was looking like she wanted to bite someone. Mr Balotelli was holding his head in his hands. And that was how I got be on TV, for the first time, not the last. GO ME!

8.

You Only Get One Shot

I hate PE when it's on the field: in a wheelchair, you're only half as mobile on grass. I'd been praying for rain for the Danny Cash training session so that we'd be in the gym but, of course, it was a sunny day. We were all set up on the football pitch, boys and girls together for a change; the goals were up (with brand new nets) and the lines had been repainted, especially for the occasion. Being on a football pitch with my heroes didn't feel real. I was shaking even more than usual with excitement and apprehension. Half of me was scared of making a fool of myself. Half of me knew this was my moment to change everything.

Mr Balotelli had joined us, but both he and Mr Marsh were mostly spectators as Mr Lustig-Prean and the footballers ran the show. The girls were in shorts or short skirts, except for the Muslim girls who wore long PE trousers. The boys were all in their PE shorts (except me – I wear tracksuit bottoms because I'm so self-conscious about my skinny white legs) but some had their Earl's Court shirts on because Mr Marsh said they could, just this once. Misbah wore his Manchester United shirt and Luca his Chelsea one. Rio's Earl's Court shirt had **Cash 9** emblazoned across the back. He had his fluorescent orange football boots on too. I had a pair of grubby trainers from Tesco.

Gary Reed said, 'You'd better be good to get away with those boots, son.'

Rio said, 'Yeah, I am.'

Danny Cash said, 'Love the shirt, mate. I'll have to sign it for you later.' And he clapped his hand across Rio's shoulders.

Mr Lustig-Prean ('Just call me Seb.' No one did) tapped his watch as he caught Danny Cash's eye.

'OK,' said Danny Cash. 'You always start with a warm-up. A good warm-up reduces your chance of injury and improves your performance. Let's kick off with some gentle stretching.'

We did. Very gentle in my case. Touching your toes isn't too challenging when you're sitting down already and taking your knee up to waist height is a doddle. Jogging then sprinting then jogging then sprinting posed more of a problem. Me and Mia shovelled ourselves around the perimeter of the pitch as best we could.

'Where the hell did you get to?' Mia hissed at me.

Before I could answer, Mrs Welbeck said, 'Now who'd like a little push?'

I whispered, 'I got hijacked; I'm sorry.' Then said, 'No thanks, we're fine,' in my loudest voice.

I wanted to get in first, before anything unfortunate came out of Mia's mouth. I smiled at her and she raised her eyebrows.

'I'll tell you later,' I said.

I can't tell you how bad we were at dribbling the football between cones. We just sat out after that while the class did their other warm-up exercises. No one had thought to make the session accessible to all of us. No one ever does.

It was interesting to watch everyone. Obviously, I watched the three footballers because they are STARS but I watched everyone else, too. I'm good at watching. I'd never seen so much effort; some of the boys were trying so hard to get signed up by Earl's Court (as if) they pretty much exhausted themselves in the warm-up. Some of the girls just wanted to hang around together and gossip and giggle and point at the STARS when they thought they couldn't be seen. Mind you, some of the girls were so athletic, they were a joy to watch (Shanika and Shannon for shtarters, sorry starters).

Danny Cash broke off from the training session

to come over to us. All muscles and self-confidence. Wow, wow, wow.

'Alright Mia, love?' he said.

'Yeah. How you doing, Uncle Danny?'

'Sound. You gotta good school here. Some decent players an' all. Who's the lad with the orange boots?'

'Rio,' said Mia, sounding bored.

'The boy's got talent. And taste, look at his shirt.'

'Don't tell him for God's sake,' said Mia. 'He thinks he's … *you* already.'

'Like I said, the boy's got taste.'

Danny Cash grinned as he ran off, legs pumping beneath his tracksuit bottoms.

'Right. We're all warmed up, some of us a bit warmer than others by the look of it. Let's do some serious training now. This is just a little taste of what we have to do every day. Nicky and Gary, in the penalty areas. Mr Marsh, can you choose two groups of seven for Nicky and Gary to work with? The other twelve kids, come and join me in the centre circle…'

Actually, there were fourteen other kids. Guess which two he hadn't counted? The two that don't count for the likes of Danny Cash, of course.

'…oh, Mia and your little mate … this is gonna be tricky for you. Maybe you could watch Nicky and Gary's groups? *Or*, I know, you two and Mrs … Mrs

Helper could get your own football and find different ways of throwing it to each other.'

Good grief: I didn't even dare look at Mia.

The kids all rushed off to their places. Mr Marsh threw a football to Mrs Welbeck, then joined Danny Cash in the centre circle. Mrs Welbeck, Mia and I were left on the sidelines.

'Come on, you, two. Who can throw the ball over their heads?'

Mia stared at Mrs Welbeck like she was going to shove the football where no one would ever see it again. Like she was going to say something *so* bad, *so* outrageously terrible that Mr Lustig-Prean would think that he'd got off lightly.

'Mia,' I said. 'NO.'

It was a risk talking to Mia like that but it worked. Mia nodded at me and gave me a horrible imitation of a smile.

'Mrs Welbeck,' she said. 'I really appreciate your help but frankly, if I never throw another ball to you or Billy again as long as I live, it will still be too soon. No offence. Me and Billy will help gather the stray balls from the other groups. Why don't you give your invaluable support to that group of girls doing nothing? They look like they could use it and they are totally messing things up for the mighty Danny Cash.'

'Well, that's charming,' said Mrs Welbeck as she turned on her heels, but I could tell she was relieved to get away from us. From Mia anyway.

'Finally, we lose the baggage,' said Mia. 'Or "The Bag", as I like to call her for short.'

'That's not very kind,' I said.

'Oh Billy, are you gonna be a goody-goody all your life? The world's still turning and the sun's still shining so don't you worry your pretty little head, eh? Listen,' said Mia, 'I've been trying to talk to you forever and I didn't want The Bag to be there. This is important stuff, Billy. For me at least. I'm sure you had a good reason for standing me up but right now I just need you to listen.'

I thought about defending Mrs Welbeck again but there was no point. She'd be The Bag for evermore, just as I'd always be Billy the Flid.

'What is it, Mia?'

Danny Cash was organising the training session in the middle of the pitch. Mia looked over at him.

'Well, this isn't easy Billy so I'm just gonna say it straight. You know that that's my Uncle Danny over there?'

'Yeah.'

'Well. There's quite a strong chance that … he's … not actually … my uncle.'

'What do you mean,' I said. 'How can you not know if you're related?'

'Did I say that we weren't related? We're definitely related and Danny and Owen Cash are definitely my uncle and my dad. It's just not … totally certain … which one is which.'

'I don't understand,' I said. 'How can you not be sure…?' I trailed off as my mind began to click the pieces into place. Did I ever mention that I can be a little slow on the uptake when it comes to relationships?

'Well, do you remember, Billy, those Year 7 science lessons, about what happens when a man and a woman love each other very much?'

Mia was still cross with me. I gritted my teeth and nodded.

'I really hope that I don't have to take you through all of that again. Let's just say that there was a whole lot of lovin' going on fourteen years ago. Maybe that's another reason my mum didn't hang around. Who knows? Anyway, by the time I was born, it was obvious that Danny was going to be the bigshot superstar and Owen was going to be the also-ran. Danny was spending his time driving fast cars and chasing women, when he wasn't playing football. There was no way he was up to bringing up a baby, let alone a Black, disabled baby with no mum. It was decided that Owen was my dad and that the club would give him money to help raise me and to keep it all out of the papers and no one would mention it again. Neat and tidy, huh?'

'Blimey, Mia. I don't…' I didn't know what to say. Could Danny Cash really not care if he was a dad or not? 'How did you find out?'

'Oh, one of my dad's more drunken evenings. He tried to deny it the next day, of course, but have you ever tried getting toothpaste back into the tube?'

'Mia,' I said. 'You need to find out for the sake of your sanity, and your Uncle Danny needs to face up to his responsibilities. That means more than just chucking a bit of money at the problem. They can do tests, can't they?'

'Thanks ever so much for telling me what I need to do, Billy,' said Mia, sarcastically.

'I don't need to,' I said. 'You know already.'

'Blimey, Billy. Since when did *you* start being the wise one?'

Beats me. Maybe it's called growing up. Mia's feisty attitude was starting to make some sense.

'Come on,' I said. 'Let's go and help.' We had to do something to be part of the training session and helping was the best I could manage at that moment.

Gary Reed and Nicky Dulgence had a training

group each in the penalty areas. There was a ball balanced on a short cone on the spot. Five kids in blue bibs were passing a ball around and trying to knock the stationary ball off. Two kids in yellow bibs were defending it. It was a great idea for developing quick passing skills and incredible defending practice. Occasionally they would swap the bibs around. I wished I could join in. Danny Cash was running some really complicated session in which three teams of four were competing against each other. I couldn't quite get the hang of it but it was obvious that (The Evil) Rio was the star. By a mile. Rio is a nasty piece of work these days but, blimey, is he ever good at football.

Danny Cash said, 'Take it steady, Rio. You'll be stealing my job at this rate.'

That's when Rio started doing tricks and every blooming one of them worked.

There were balls flying everywhere so me and Mia had plenty of work to do, scooping them up and chucking them back. It was better than playing catch between ourselves anyway and at least we were a small part of the action. Not exactly what I had been hoping for though.

Mr Lustig-Prean said, 'Well done, wheelchair guys. You're being really helpful.'

Some of Mia's swear words leapt into my head but

I would never use them. Well, only at Nettle. Or Rio. I looked at Mia to see if she was going to say something but she was gazing into the distance, she clearly had other things on her mind. I could guess what.

We actually managed to get involved in one of the five-a-side games Danny Cash organised next. Some of the girls didn't want to join in so they were a player short. This was my moment.

I said, 'Me and Mia can be in goal.'

And this time nobody laughed. We even made a couple of good saves and it felt awesome. Mr Lustig-Prean made sure that the photographers got some good shots of us.

Danny Cash said, 'Nice one, Mia.'

She ignored him. Lustig-Prean tapped his watch.

'OK,' said Danny Cash. 'That's nearly it, kids. You've been amazing. We might even have one or two future Earl's Court players here I reckon.'

Gary Reed and Nicky Dulgence nodded unconvincingly while Danny Cash mouthed 'you' at Rio before carrying on. 'But I'm afraid it's time we got back to our training ground.'

There was a mass 'Awwwwww', the like of which I hadn't heard since primary school.

'But there's one more thing,' said Danny Cash as Mr Lustig-Prean handed him an envelope.

'Thanks, L-P. In here, I've got two pairs of tickets to watch Earl's Court's next home game, this Saturday, best seats in the house.'

The derby! A buzz went around the class. This was the biggest game of the season.

'Two of you,' said Danny Cash, 'are gonna be bringing a mate or your dad or whoever, to see me, Nicky, Gary and the lads stuff Chelsea.'

The footballers all smiled as a cheer went up from all of the kids, even the Chelsea fans.

'What's the score gonna be, Danny?' said Rio. First name terms already. Of course.

'I reckon 5–0, Rio, with yet another hat-trick for the boy Cash,' said the boy Cash.

'If selected,' said Gary Reed, and Danny Cash shot him a dirty look.

'I don't think there's much doubt about that, is there?' said Danny Cash. 'Not for me anyway. I could always have a word with the Gaffer about you, though.'

'So, who gets 'em, Danny? Who gets the tickets?' said Rio. 'The best footballer or the kid with the best shirt?'

'The boy and the girl,' said Danny Cash, 'who can score the best goal. Simple as that. You'll be playing with me. Everybody gets their chance but you only get one shot at goal. I'll be supplying the killer, final pass, Nicky will be defending and Gary will be in goal. We'll take it one at a time. Why don't you go first, Rio? We'll show everyone how it's done. We start on the halfway line.'

I'd crawl over hot coals to get to that game. In fact, any game. There's no way me and Mum can afford match tickets. Maybe if we sold Nettle? Maybe not.

So, how was Billy the Flid going to pull this one off? Simple, all I had to do was learn how to run and kick a ball in the next twenty seconds. In the bag.

Or … what would Mia be thinking? This is it. This is the chance. Whatever it takes; this is the moment your life changes. Finally, opportunity trumped fear.

9.

My Mate Rio

'Right,' said Danny Cash. 'Mr Balotelli is the ref and the sole judge of which two kids score the best goals. One boy, one girl. No arguments. Dissent is punishable with a red card. Rio, you're up first. Set a high standard, mate.'

Rio positioned himself in the centre circle while Danny Cash went wide right with a football under his arm. Nicky Dulgence blocked his path to goal.

'You ready, Rio?'

Rio nodded and Danny Cash put the ball down.

'Let's go.'

Watching his skill close up, not just on TV, was astonishing. Danny Cash turned Nicky Dulgence this way and that, making himself space and laying the ball off to Rio who kept it long enough to draw the solitary defender towards him, before knocking it back. Danny Cash was now free to bomb down the right wing and he did. Rio made a parallel run through the middle. The cross, when it came in, was pinpoint. Rio met it on the volley with his right foot and the ball nestled in the back of the net before Gary Reed had a chance to move.

Rio whooped in triumph and raised his arms. Danny Cash ran towards him and began a complicated dance routine which Rio mirrored, rather more gracefully. Danny's chunky legs aren't made for dancing. They finished with a double high-five and a brief embrace.

'I think we might have our winner already,' said Danny Cash as Rio strutted around, nodding.

The applause that had broken out when Rio scored was long dead. Kids just stared sullenly at the two preening peacocks, me included. Beat that, Billy. Yeah right.

'That ain't fair,' said Scott and, for once, I agreed with him.

'You're right,' said Danny Cash. 'Come and score a better one.'

Scott tried but he couldn't even hit the net. Neither could Orla, Shannon, Yakubu, Maysoon, Tyrell, Shanika or Liam.

Jordan hammered a great shot wide of the post into Mr Balotelli's 'breadbasket' as they say. Elisha, Misbah, Luca, Adedoja and Tomasz all scored good goals, but nowhere near as brilliant as Rio. Jaz, Junaid and Precious all missed their shots completely. Hisham mis-hit the ball straight into his own face and looked like he wanted to cry. Rio laughed an awful lot at nearly every effort.

Eboni controlled a tricky cross from Danny Cash, dummied Gary Reed in goal, left him on his backside and rolled the ball into the empty net. It was quality and even Rio clapped.

Tyreece is a brilliant player but the cross went a metre over his head.

Danny Cash just said, 'You should've gone far post, mate.'

Rio laughed some more while Tyreece glared.

The rest of the kids decided not to have a go. They either realised that they were hopeless at football or they knew there was no way they could beat Rio and Eboni.

Mia turned to me and said, 'Notice how nobody's asked us yet.'

'Not even Uncle Daddy, I mean Danny,' I said. I was getting bold with Mia.

'Whatever,' she said wearily.

'Let's be honest, though,' I said. 'How on earth are we supposed to score a goal?'

'Well, maybe my legs don't work but last time I looked in the mirror, I still had a head. Ah sod it,

Uncle Danny can always get me in if I want. I don't need to win the tickets anyway.'

I did, and Mia had got me thinking.

'Maybe they'll ask us when the other kids have finished,' I said. You know, it's amazing; I don't care about my squeaky voice when I talk to Mia. And I don't squeak so much.

'Fat chance,' said Mia and she was right.

Once all the other kids had either had a go or sat out, Mr Lustig-Prean said, 'Right, let's see what the teachers can do before we give those tickets out. Mr Balotelli?'

Mr B doesn't *do* football and he didn't look confident. Danny Cash skinned Nicky Dulgence one more time and laid the ball into my tutor's path. Mr Balotelli began dribbling towards goal with a terrified look on his face as Nicky Dulgence caught him up.

When he reached the edge of the penalty area, Danny Cash yelled, 'TO ME,' just as he was about to shoot.

Mr B swung his foot and looked up in panic at the same time. You can probably guess the result. The ball dribbled into Gary Reed's arms; Mr Balotelli's right shoe went over the crossbar. Danny Cash looked up at the sky, rolled his eyes and cussed. Mr B ended up on his backside with even less respect from his tutor group than he had before.

Mr Marsh stepped forward, shaking his head. 'My turn, I think.'

He picked up the ball and said to the footballers, 'We're not all muppets.' As he stared contemptuously at Mr Balotelli on the ground.

'I used to be on the books at Brentford, you know.'

'*Really*?' said Nicky Dulgence.

'*Wow*!' said Danny Cash, and they sniggered behind his back, just like we do.

It was a set-up really. Mr Marsh (in his shortest, tightest shorts) started running from the halfway line. Danny Cash crossed the ball into his path but so slowly that Nicky Dulgence reached the ball at the same time as Mr Marsh. They call it a hospital pass; there was only going to be one result. The England defender went in hard at knee height, with all his weight behind him. Mr Marsh (not a small man) was instantly rendered horizontal and seemed to be suspended a metre off the ground, like in a cartoon. Fresh air doesn't hold you for long. Mr Marsh belly-flopped into the ground with an awful expulsion of air as Nicky Dulgence slid right beneath him.

'Fair tackle,' said Mr Balotelli, as Nicky Dulgence jumped up and pumped fists with Danny Cash.

'OK,' said Mr Lustig-Prean as Mr Marsh staggered

away, muttering bad things and glaring at Mr Balotelli. 'Time to give out those tickets.'

I could feel my heart pound against my ribs. I could *hear* the blood inside my ears.

'What about me?' I said. The words hung in the air like a fart at a tea party. I must be mad. What was I thinking? I felt like I was rolling into a black hole but I had to do it. I had to show them. I had literally dragged myself through mud to get here. There was no way I was going to miss this moment.

Rio and Danny Cash started to laugh but stopped when they realised that no one else was.

'Oh, you're serious,' said Danny Cash. There was silence for ages. 'No offence mate, but how are you gonna score a goal?'

I said, 'Yeah, I'm serious, Danny.'

Wow, it felt good.

'Danny, I'm sure I don't need to tell *you* that you can score with any part of your body except for your arms. Are you good enough to cross the ball at my head height?'

He looked a little offended. 'Yeah, course I am.'

'Well,' I said. 'I'm going to ask my mate Rio to help me.'

Even Mia was looking at me like I was mad, now.

'Billy…' she whispered.

Rio was stood there with his mouth open. Literally. Lower jaw hanging, lips parted like a Venus Fly Trap.

'Rio mate, do you remember at dinner time,' I said, 'when we were messing around and you were seeing how fast you could push me?'

Rio stared at me disbelievingly. I was making it up at high speed as I went along. I had never, never spoken more than a short sentence before in front of an audience. They were hanging on my words, no one was laughing. It felt great.

'Well, I want you to push me *as fast as you can* straight at the near post. Danny, I'm relying on you to beat your man and put the ball on my head. I know you can do it. OK Rio? Let's go.'

Mia put her hand on my shoulder (omigod, she touched me) and whispered, 'Billy, if you pull this off then you are spaz of the century but whatever happens, I think you're great.'

And that simple sentence, ugly word and all, was the best thing I had ever heard. The most beautiful poetry. The words that changed my life. It made me feel like I could do anything. Like I was Superman. I nearly ran to the starting place on the halfway line.

But I didn't. Rio pushed me there *after* running up to Danny Cash and saying something apparently hilarious into his ear and *while* leaning forward and telling me, 'Those tickets are mine, spaz, and you know it. This ain't about you. Don't even think about trying to make me look stupid. I'm gonna push you fast alright. I'm gonna push you faster than you've ever been pushed before and I'm gonna mash you right into that goalpost and then I'm gonna say, "oh, sorry Billy MATE. I was only trying to help." No raspberry's gonna make a monkey out of me. Ya get me?'

We used to giggle together at primary school. Me and Rio. We used to play Top Trumps and make silly jokes and laugh until we'd forgotten what we were laughing about. Now he wanted to 'mash' me. My plan was looking dodgy and my confidence was evaporating like the sweat on my brow. Danny Cash made his way to the wing. Me and Rio waited on the halfway line. I looked at Mia; she was smiling and biting her lip at the same time.

Danny Cash put the ball down. 'GO,' he said.

Nicky Dulgence shepherded him towards the sideline. Danny Cash did two stepovers and gained half a yard. Rio started pushing me like he was possessed.

Nicky Dulgence tried to recover but was wrong-footed and Danny Cash sprinted past him, down the line. Me and Rio were picking up speed too in midfield, ten metres now from the box. Nicky Dulgence was beaten and Danny Cash made for the byline. Rio got up to full speed which, blimey, is *fast*. I gripped my armrests.

Rio was breathing heavily and he hissed, 'You're gonna die, spastic,' as we hurtled into the penalty area.

I thought my heart would jump out of my ribcage; it was beating so hard. Danny Cash crossed the ball as the wind screamed alarms in my ears and the near post got rapidly nearer.

10.

Superman

'It wasn't looking good, Net,' I said and the little hairball cocked her head so far to one side it looked like it might just snap off.

'I was beginning to think I was nuts, getting Rio to push me but I knew that he could do it fast, which I needed, and I really wanted to get him back for dumping me in the woods. Is that childish? Maybe, but I showed them, Net. I showed them what I CAN do.'

Nettle winked and groaned like a creaky door.

'I'll take that as a "yes", but he had it coming, you've got to give me that.'

I'd been expecting a call or a text from Mia but there had been nothing yet. Should I call her? I didn't know how these things worked.

'When Danny Cash crossed the ball in, he put it low. You know, I reckon he might have crossed low on purpose because he thinks my legs don't work at all but I've got other bits. I bet that's what him and Rio were laughing about. Anyway, that's when Rio said, "go on then, spaz", and I did. Super-spaz. Half a second away from smashing into the goalpost, I launched myself sideways, out of my chair, with all my strength. Just like in the woods. The chair tipped up and Rio fell over it, cursing. I fell head-first towards the ball. Rio shouted bad words. I saw my chance. Everything seemed to be in slow motion. Just before I clattered into the ground like a bag of bones, I got my forehead to the ball. Perfect technique. PERFECT TECHNIQUE, Nettle. Lionel Messi couldn't have bettered it. The diving header flew past Gary Reed, into the far corner. Goal of the Season.

'I didn't see cos I was rolling in the dirt but I could tell I'd scored because everyone was cheering. I banged my head and twisted my arm, but I don't care. My wheelchair has still got mud and grass in the nooks and crannies. I don't want to wash it but I bet Mum makes me. Mr Balotelli said, "I think we have our winner – Billy Turpin!" and I have never felt so happy, Nettle. *Never*. Mr B and Mrs Welbeck helped me back into my chair and Mrs Welbeck told me off while Rio said stuff like, "that ain't fair, sir" and "that ain't no goal – he fouled me" although how you can foul someone on your own team, I don't know. I did it, Nettle. I DID IT!'

Nettle jumped up and tried to lick me. She likes to

get her tongue in my mouth but I don't let her. I know where she's been.

'I can't believe it, Net. I'm going to the Chelsea game on Saturday. I'd love to take you, littl'un but I'm taking Mum.'

Mum's really excited and she says she's proud of me.

'I've got to tell some people, Net,' I said, logging on to my laptop. 'I know it's boasting but I don't care.'

A young Danny Cash smiled back at me from the screen. I'd set this picture as my background years ago, but I didn't want it anymore. I changed it for a posed photo of the whole ECFC squad. My eyes wandered then to the picture of Danny Cash behind my desk. It was a famous shot of him in mid-air, halfway through an overhead bicycle kick that sent the ball into the top corner of the net against Manchester City. I've never met a hero before but he really didn't seem so heroic anymore. Maybe I love the idea of Danny Cash more than the person. Maybe I was feeling like a bit of a hero myself. I don't know. I took that picture and seven more of him down and put them carefully in my drawer in case I changed my mind. That left just fifteen. It felt like a good compromise.

I went to my favourite site first and posted the whole story. I think I might have been gloating, just a little bit. I know that's not good but I couldn't resist it. I needed to play some more football so I gently shoved Nettle off my lap – growling of course – and moved onto my Xbox: Earl's Court v Chelsea. I played centre-forward and I had Danny Cash playing 'in the hole' to support me but, annoyingly, he scored three and I only got one in our 4–0 victory. I told myself it's not about personal glory, it's a team game, as I raised my arms to acknowledge the adulation of the crowd. OK, the sullen glaring of Nettle.

My mum knocked on the door and called, 'Billy love, I'm off out now.'

'What? You never said.'

My mum opened the door and put her head around it. 'I did, babes, you weren't listening. Your head's all full of this football malarkey.'

I couldn't argue.

'You are coming on Saturday, aren't you?'

'I wouldn't miss it, babes. Now I've got to rush.'

'Where you going, Mum?'

'A date.'

'Already?' I said. 'He's keen.'

'I hope so,' said my mum. 'His name's Mike. This is our second date.'

'Oh, have fun.'

'I will. School tomorrow, bed by ten, yeah?'

'Yeah, yeah.'

Her perfume lingered long after she had closed the door and made Nettle sneeze.

'I know, Nettle,' I said. 'Let's hope it has the same effect on her new bloke.'

That's when my mobile rang (the Champions League anthem). I knew who it was and my heart rate seemed to double. What was *that* about?

'**Billy's phone – ANSWER**. Hi Mia,' I said, trying not to breathe too heavily.

'Hey superstar,' said Mia, only gently taking the mick. 'How's the Phil Foden of Willesden Junction doing?'

'Ah Mia,' I said. 'I just can't take it in. It's not just getting the tickets. It's winning them in front of the whole tutor group…'

'And beating bloody Rio.'

'…and beating bloody Rio.'

You know, once you start swearing, it gets a lot easier. I guess it's like anything else, you just need to practise.

'Listen Billy, I've only got a minute; my dad's not having a brilliant evening. I just wanted to say well done. I am *so* proud of you. Not just because you're the first wheelchair user in the history of wheelchair users to score a goal with a diving header but because of your guts. I didn't know you had it in you, spaz-bag. I thought you were nuts mind, getting Rio to push you.'

'Mia, I've said before, I don't like you calling me that. Anyway, I was so angry with Rio,' I said. 'I didn't get the chance to tell you. Rio and Hisham dumped me out of my chair in the woods, trying to make me miss the footballers. I'm really sorry but I was crawling through the woods when I was supposed to be meeting you. I hate Rio. I wanted to get him back.'

'*That's* where you got to. I couldn't think what you were doing. Blimey Billy, remind me never to get you angry.'

Actually, Mia often makes me angry but it's OK, somehow. Here's an example:

'So,' she said. 'You got back into your chair. *By yourself.* You got back through the woods. *By yourself.* You got back to class, stole Danny Cash's thunder and made a fool out of Rio. *By yourself.* Remind me, Billy. What do you need Mrs Wel … sorry, The Bag for?'

I couldn't answer, so I changed the subject. I said, 'Do you think Rio's gonna be *really* angry?'

'He's gonna be furious. What do you care?'

Through all the euphoria at getting the tickets, I was scared of how Rio might react. I knew he would have most of the class on his side so, what had it all been for?

I said, 'He might dump me in the woods again.'

'And you know you can get back.'

'What if he takes my wheelchair next time?'

'Then crawl.'

'What if he beats me up?'

'Then run him over in your chair. Bite his ankles till he stops. I don't know, Billy. What's happened to Billy Turpin, superhero? You can beat him, Billy. You've proved it. You've proved it to all of them and, more importantly, you've proved it to yourself. Now, it's time to take on the world.'

'Yeah, right,' I said.

'I mean it. You can do whatever you want, Billy. That's gotta be a great feeling.'

It did feel good doing stuff for myself but I definitely didn't have Mia's confidence. Yet.

'I'm not *you*, Mia,' I said.

'No, you're not. You should feel very happy that you're *you*, Billy. Really. Do you think I never get scared? Sometimes I don't even know how I get out of bed. I want to curl up until the bad stuff goes away, but sometimes you just gotta fake it to make it.'

'What on earth does *that* mean?'

'It means you gotta grow up. It means you gotta do the things that are hard and scary because each time you do, it's a little bit less hard and scary the next time. No, you're not me, Billy. I reckon you're a whole load stronger. I reckon that for a frightened little raspberry, you're pretty bleedin' fab.'

Pretty bleedin' fab. She thinks I'm pretty bleedin' fab! I heard a faint shout of 'Mia' in the background.

'Listen, I gotta go. I'll see you tomorrow, Superman.'

'See you, Mia.'

I said, '**Billy's phone – END CALL**' and looked long and hard at Nettle.

Is Mia my girlfriend? How can you tell?

'Wow,' I said, and I sat and ran the conversation over in my head for ages before turning to my laptop.

There was a new DM. Back to the scary world.

who dya fink u r mong –
yer dead meat bruv ya get me

11.

Hiding Behind a Girly

Sometimes you wake up and it just feels like every other time you've woken up and you know that the day will be the same old same old. Sometimes, just occasionally, everything seems different.

My eyes opened before my alarm went off and my brain seemed to hit the ground running (I know, I know). I think it must have been working on stuff before I woke up. I thought about what Mia had said and how Danny Cash might be her dad. I thought about my wonder-goal and how everyone would look at me differently now. I thought about *the match* on Saturday and how amazing that would be. I thought about that horrible threat I'd got last night and who could have sent it. Hmmm, who uses phrases like 'mong' and 'dead meat' and 'ya get me'? It was a puzzler. I thought about how full my bladder was feeling and that thought trumps all others, apparently.

I used to use this special, 'night-toilet' contraption

(you don't need the details) and it still stands by the side of my bed, but I've been getting stronger and better at looking after myself and now I'm not going to use it anymore. It makes me feel like a little kid, and anyway, it can't be any fun for my mum having to empty it. I thought about what Mia would say and shuddered; you can bet your bottom dollar she hasn't got one in her bedroom. I have plans to ask her around sometime and it would definitely have to go before *that* happened.

I hauled myself into my chair and made my way to the bathroom. There're handles attached to each side of the toilet and I can use my upper body strength to get on and off. Maria, one of my online friends with CP, told me a horror story about how she fell while doing this and had to be rescued by her dad. It didn't bear thinking about, so I made a plan to work even harder with my physio.

❦

I washed my hands and opened the door. Nettle sleeps in the kitchen and the door is supposed to be closed, but she was out and trying to jump into my lap.

'Hi hairy, what you doing out here?' I said, like she could answer. Nettle bounced on her hind legs, her tongue flicking in and out in anticipation of a kiss.

'I love you, Nettle, but not in that way. Now bog off cos I need my breakfast.' She looked vaguely hurt but I reckoned she'd get over it.

It sounded like Mum was getting up too. I heard her bedroom door open and close as I put Nettle down on the floor. I wanted to talk to her about cleaning all my Earl's Court gear (shirt, hat, scarf, undies) before Saturday. Nettle started barking.

I rolled into the hall expecting to see Mum but instead there was a man, a strange man, leaving through the front door. Tall and wearing (old person's) going-out clothes. He looked awkward.

'Hi, you must be Billy,' he said. 'I'm Mike. I'm just leaving but I'm pleased to meet you. I don't think your dog likes me very much, by the way. I'll see you around.'

Nettle moved two steps towards him, growling, then four steps back. She really isn't that brave. Mike closed the door before I had a chance to say anything. Before I had a chance to get my jaw off the floor. Once it was closed, Nettle rushed the door barking wildly. I stared blankly at the peeling paint on the panelling, like *that* was going to enlighten me. Mike? This had never happened before.

'Morning, Billy love,' said Mum coming out of the bedroom. She was wearing her old dressing gown and her hair was all over the shop. 'Did you—'

'See Mike?' I said. 'Oh yes, I saw Mike. Mike said "hi". Mike knew my name. Mike seems a nice guy. Who the heck is Mike?'

'Billy. Please don't talk to me like that. Mike is my … boyfriend.'

Like Mia's my girlfriend?

'Since when?'

'I've known Mike for some time. We've been close for … a while.'

A while? Boy, my wheels can turn slowly sometimes but a thought was forming in my head.

'I wasn't expecting to see him…'

'I know love. I should have said something.'

'Yeah.' I felt a little foolish. 'I'm sorry if I was rude, Mum. I was just expecting to see you. Not … Mike.'

'Billy, you're a lovely boy,' said my mum, bending down and hugging me. 'I think we might be seeing a little more of Mike.'

I had to say it. 'Mum, is Mike … my dad?'

Mum has always been really cagey about my dad. She never really told me anything except that he had left us when I was a baby.

'Oh Billy. No love, he's not. I'm sorry babes but your dad is probably the most selfish man on the planet. He's really, really NOT a very nice person and there is no way I would *ever* let him back into our lives. Not that he'd want to anyway.'

Mum put her hands on my shoulders and looked me in the eye. 'Your dad, Billy, only ever did one good thing in his life and that was to help bring you into this world. After that input, we're all well shot of him, trust me. Your dad's long gone, my love, and that's a very good thing.'

'So, what on earth were you doing with him, Mum?'

'That's a question I've asked myself many times, Billy,' Mum said. 'The thing is, you don't get to choose who you fall for.'

I wanted to tell Mum about Mia, but I didn't. We had another hug and I went to get ready for school.

I was looking forward to school. Mostly, anyway. Looking forward to seeing Mia and looking forward to basking in my new-found hero status.

I arrived at my tutor group, ready to receive my acclaim. I was greeted by a tsunami of indifference, and a few smaller waves of outright hostility. I saw mostly the backs of people's heads. Mia smiled briefly, then carried on talking to Eboni and Shanika. Rio gave me his hard stare. Hisham grinned unpleasantly.

Mr Balotelli said, 'Good morning, Billy. We're just about to start. Could you find a seat quickly please?'

I raised my eyebrows and he said, 'You know what I mean.'

Someone blew a raspberry as I found a space, nowhere near Mia, and there was some sniggering. Not quite the open-top bus tour I'd been expecting then.

Hardly a soul spoke to me until morning break. In the corridor on the way to English, Mia whispered briefly, 'Could be a rough one, Billy. Rio's been getting to them, and his cronies. We were right; he's not happy. Just rise above it.'

A couple of the boys told me I was a lucky so and so – or words to that effect – and Hisham told me I'd stolen Rio's tickets. None of the girls offered to push me between lessons and most of them were being really mean to Eboni as well, although not Mia.

The morning seemed awfully long. In the playground at break, I told Mia about Mike.

'So, your mum's moving on then,' she said. 'Good for her.'

'What do you mean, "good for her"?' I said. 'My mum's bringing strange men into the flat.'

'How many strange men?'

'Well, Mike.'

'One then. In all your thirteen years. Look Billy, your mum's done nothing wrong and let's be honest here, at least you know who your mum is.'

'Yeah, and you know who your dad is…' I so wished I hadn't started that sentence, '…roughly.'

'Hmmm, roughly,' said Mia, she paused. 'Yeah, that's what every kid needs. Abandoned by her mum and allocated a dad on the toss of a coin. Tails you lose, Owen Cash. Just great.' And she turned her wheelchair away from me. Her shoulders started shaking.

Nice one, Billy. I'd never made a girl cry before. Maybe Mia's not quite as tough as she makes out. I didn't know what to do so I put my hand on her armrest and gently turned her towards me.

'Mia, I'm…' I began and that's as far as I got.

'Don't touch my wheelchair,' said Mia and her eyes scared me to my soul. Back in control of herself, apparently.

'I'm sorry, Mia,' I said.

I tell you what, I was one sorry raspberry, but at least we had eye contact again. In the soap operas, this is where they say, 'I know how you must feel' and the other person always replies, 'how can you possibly know how I feel?'

I wanted to avoid that so I just said, 'We've been dealt a pretty rubbish hand of parents, haven't we?'

'Billy,' she said. 'There's lots worse off than us.'

'I know. But it's always been just me and Mum, you know?'

'Maybe you're due a bit of change then. Give Mike a chance.'

'Yeah.'

I smiled and put my hand on Mia's arm. She stared at it until I took it away again. Maybe she's not quite my girlfriend yet. I felt it was time to change the subject.

'You won't believe what I was sent last night.'

'A virtual poke from a virtual person that's of virtually no interest?'

'A death threat, Mia. A real, live death threat. "Yer dead meat bruv," it said. And they called me a mong.'

'Blimey, Billy, what's that about? Who was it?'

'I don't know, it was some made-up name: "H-bom" or something. Why would anyone hate *me* so much?'

'It's not just about hate, is it? It's about power. Some saddo, sat behind a screen, spoiling other people's lives without ever having to stand up and be counted. What did you do? You didn't answer it, did you?'

'No,' I said. 'But I'm thinking about it.'

'Don't,' said Mia. 'Don't give them the satisfaction. If you reply, they'll know they've got to you. They've wielded their power then, haven't they? Just screenshot it and note the time and date you received it. Just in case. Then delete it and block the sender. They'll probably get bored.'

I thought people would think differently about me after that goal. It just seemed to have made things worse.

'It's Rio. I know it is. What if he means it?'

'Billy, it could be anyone. It could be any one of the kids, it could be The Bag, it could be Mr Balotelli. It could be me. It could be someone you've never met. You just don't know.'

'It's Rio,' I said. 'He finished with, "ya get me" just like Rio says.'

'And a million other people. Not just Rio. You just don't know. Listen, whoever it is, they want to get into your head, so don't let them. If they haven't even got the courage to threaten you in person, I don't think you're in too much danger, but if it carries on then we're telling someone.'

'We are?'

'Ye-eah! It's probably someone at school, Billy. School has to sort this stuff out, as well as what happened in the woods yesterday, and if they can't, the police need to know. It's just not on. If it's in school it's bullying which isn't allowed; if it's outside of school, it's threatening behaviour which is illegal. Either way, it's got to stop and you don't have to put up with it.'

Rio and a few of his mates walked past. Someone

blew a raspberry and there was the usual sniggering. I made sure I kept my eyes down. Mia didn't.

'That's mature, and so original,' she said. 'Which one of you losers wants to do that to my face? Or are you all too sad?'

Oh Lord. They stopped. Rio, Liam, Tyreece, Hisham and Tyrell.

'Take it steady, Mia,' said Rio. 'That wasn't aimed at you.'

Oh great.

'Sounds like it was from where I'm sat,' said Mia. 'But if you wanna dis my mate, you dis me an' all. So come on, which of you big brave boys has got something to say?'

'Bruv,' said Hisham, looking at me. 'You hiding behind a girly now?' He shook his head in disgust. I made sure I didn't catch his eye.

Rio said something really nasty under his breath about 'spending spaz-time together' and there was laughter as they swaggered off.

Mia said, 'What a bunch of complete...' and I couldn't help agreeing with her as one of the departing ... so and sos said something about a DM that I couldn't quite catch.

12.

My First Match

OK, this was it. The business. My entire life had been building up to this moment: match day. I could feel every millilitre of blood as it coursed around my body, making me buzz.

The shiny yellow and blue carapace of the Wang's Tofu Arena (Earl's Court's home ground) loomed closer as my mum and I made our way up the world-famous Easi-Noodle Boulevard, towards the life-size, bronze statue of Simon Cowell, our most famous fan.

It doesn't get better than this. Half an hour before kick-off in the derby that could decide who plays in the Champions League next season; dressed head to toe in blue and yellow. Right down to my socks and undies.

A rowdy group of Chelsea fans walked through us, shoulder to shoulder, clapping and singing. It made my heartbeat even faster but they were quickly surrounded by police who moved them on.

A tout shouted, 'Match tickets bought and sold,' when the police had gone by. 'Best prices you'll find.'

I already had my ticket. It was safe in my mum's purse and I wouldn't have sold it for anything. A thought came into my head that maybe my classmates would want to hear about the match and I had a vision of them in a circle around me, hanging on every word. Just as quickly, I realised that it didn't seem to matter so much anymore and that I should just enjoy the match for what it was.

Hotdog vendors lined the way along with men selling programmes and blue and yellow scarves and flags that read 'COME ON YOU EARLS'. We'd all be singing that soon. I'd heard it on the telly and I couldn't wait.

I asked Mum for a programme and a hotdog and she said, 'Put it this way, Billy. You can have a programme and a hotdog, or we can eat for the next fortnight.'

I didn't think I'd get them, but I thought it might add to the experience and it's always worth a try.

There was a sudden flurry of shouting behind us and some of the younger fans ran around the back of the Nelson Mandela Stand (he was our second most famous fan), chased by more police. I think that's where that group of Chelsea fans had gone. It just couldn't be any more exciting.

Entering the ground, a female steward searched

my mum and a male one searched me. I felt a weird thrill that they thought I might be a hooligan with a concealed weapon.

Mr Lustig-Prean had arranged for us to be seated in the accessible area, almost on the halfway line, in front of the stand and behind the advertising hoardings. An incredible spot. Next to the managers' technical areas and the benches where the substitutes sit. Oh-My-God.

I heard the familiar tones of the theme music to *The Apprentice* start up, the music Earl's Court always run out to. It's so much louder when you're there than it is on *Match of the Day* or Sky Sports. The officials were first out, followed by Danny Cash and the Chelsea captain, leading their teams out. Little hairs were standing up all over my body. I felt like I was crawling with insects. I really needed the toilet even though I went before we came out but I wasn't missing this for anything. I'd sooner wet meself.

The Chelsea team looked huge, muscular, confident. Some of the Earl's Court players looked like kids in comparison, like they were the Chelsea team's mascots.

There was shouting all around me: some of it encouragement, some of it just abuse. I found myself joining in, using language I'd never normally use, especially in front of my mum. I shot her a nervous glance but she was doing the same. Chelsea had only been given two thousand tickets but their fans were making an amazing noise. You could see the players on the pitch, soaking up the atmosphere: some of them nervous, some of them pumped. Danny Cash looked like a wild dog in a cage.

The handshakes were perfunctory, no smiles, no matey words. It was tense. The players took their positions on the pitch and the crowd noise became a crescendo, building up to the kick-off. The man in black raised the whistle to his lips and blew.

And everything changed. Chelsea passed the ball among themselves and then they passed it some more. They passed like it was a knockabout in the park: along the back line, into midfield, out wide, back to the full back, then the keeper, into the back line again … we couldn't get a sniff. Danny Cash chased the ball, fruitlessly, like a dog in the park. Like me when I was Piggy in the Middle. Earl's Court got the ball briefly and immediately lost it again. Danny Cash dropped deep and clattered into the back of a Chelsea midfielder. Free kick, lecture from the ref. Lucky it wasn't a booking. Muttered cusses as he walked away and the Chelsea fans jeered. I was quiet now, like all the home fans. We were being played off the park.

Earl's Court were asleep for the free kick. Chelsea swept unchallenged down the left, the yellow shirts always trailing behind the blue. A straightforward cross cleared a static defence and a Chelsea head made it 1–0 from a few metres out. Too easy. The Chelsea bench leapt to their feet, whooping and hugging. They were so close I could hear them; I could smell them.

We lost the ball almost straight from the kick-off and the same pattern started up again. The Chelsea fans started singing, 'Can we play you every week?' It was painful.

After fifteen minutes Chelsea scored again, with ease. They almost seemed to be scoring at will. Some of the Earl's Court players started to look dispirited, some still chased the ball like men possessed, led by Danny Cash. He'd gone an awful colour and his thinning hair was plastered to his head.

With ten minutes to go until half-time, Chelsea scored a third, a simple tap-in after a defensive mix-up. Embarrassing. This was turning into a disaster. And that's when Danny Cash showed why he is captain of Earl's Court and England. The Chelsea midfield dwelt on the ball for a split second too long. Danny Cash took man and ball at the same time and the whistle didn't blow. He sprayed the ball wide right to Nicky Dulgence and the whole crowd rose to their feet (well, you know, except me) sensing a goal. Sensing a turning point in the game. Danny Cash hurtled through the heart of the Chelsea defence, yelling for the return ball. It came and it was perfect. One touch off the thigh to control it, one swing of the opposite boot and the ball was in the back of the net. Genius. Nearly as good as mine. The home crowd went berserk; I was screaming randomly. Danny Cash raced into the goal to pick the ball up and started running back to the centre circle. No time to lose.

Which was when he, and we, saw the linesman's raised flag. It was *so not offside* but it went to VAR and we knew the outcome. The goal wouldn't stand. The ref was stood fifteen metres in front of me and Danny Cash bore down upon him, mouth twisted, veins bulging, eyes popping. The ref slowly backed away while Danny Cash, still holding the ball, let loose a torrent of abuse into his face. I was screaming at him too. So was Mum. So was everyone around us.

They don't change their minds. The ref just shook his head and started running backwards. Danny Cash dropped the ball onto his right foot and hammered it in pure temper.

Danny Cash's thighs make Mr Marsh's look like chicken drumsticks. When he hammers the ball, as they say, it stays hammered. It flew from his boot into the crowd. More accurately, it flew from his boot towards me. Even more accurately, it flew from his boot, into me. Naturally. The ball was travelling way too fast for me to react. It just scraped the top of the advertising hoarding and careered, no crashed, no smashed into my face.

And that was the end of my first match. The lights went out and my mum says I was knocked clean out of my wheelchair by the force of the blow. She says that Danny Cash just turned on his heel and carried on cussing, but Gary Reed came over to us, saw me unconscious with blood on my face and immediately called the Earl's Court physio over to help me. The St. John's Ambulance people took over and I can't remember much, but they must have got me into the ambulance.

The doctor in hospital said that Danny Cash's kick had broken my nose, given me concussion, a severe nosebleed and two black eyes. She said I would have to stay in overnight for observation and that my mum could stay with me. The nurse gave me some painkillers and they really did the job.

I watched *Match of the Day* from my hospital bed. We lost 4–0 in the end. Our worst result of the season. Gary Lineker said that the result was irrelevant because of the Danny Cash tantrum, which was a shocking incident that had brought shame on the

England captain and on football itself. They showed it over and over again, zooming in on the bloodied, unconscious lad on the ground. Alan Shearer said that this was the latest in a series of regrettable incidents and that Danny Cash needed to consider his position as Earl's Court and England captain. Gary Lineker said that the police would be looking into the matter.

I know I should have been angry but this was awesome: I got to be on telly *again* and not just the local news, but on the national news and on *Match of the Day*!

I went to sleep battered and blissfully happy. When I woke up, my mum was still there.

She said, 'Morning Sleeping Beauty. How you feeling?'

She had some newspapers on her lap. The top one was the *Mail on Sunday*. Its headline read, 'Is football out of control?' above two photos: one of me, all bloody on the ground, and one of Danny Cash's face, contorted in anger.

'I don't know, Mum,' I said, feeling my face. 'Sore, and I can't breathe properly.'

'This'll cheer you up,' she said. 'We've only had a phone call from Earl's Court FC, haven't we? Some bloke called Seb Lusty Prune?'

13.

Raspberryball

'Mr Lusty-Prune,' said my mum, 'wished to apologise on behalf of Earl's Court Football Club.'

I thought about putting her straight on Mr Lustig-Prean's real name but I preferred her version.

'Mr Lusty-Prune,' she continued, 'said that it was a highly unfortunate accident that has deeply upset Danny Cash. He said that replays clearly show that Danny Cash was merely trying to return the ball to a Chelsea player, so that they could take their free kick. He unfortunately, slightly misjudged his attempted pass which lobbed over the advertising and hit you, causing you to lose your balance. He thinks you must have sustained your injuries when you fell, perhaps on your wheelchair.'

Do me a favour. Both of my eyes were nearly closed because of the bruising but if I could have opened them wide in amazement and disbelief, I would have done.

'He says, although it was clearly an accident,

Danny Cash is distraught to think that he might have inadvertently contributed in any way to your injuries and would like to come here today to personally apologise.'

Again, wow. But it was only a small wow, really. The thought of another Danny Cash visit wasn't nearly so exciting as it had been. Still pretty cool though, so I said it, 'Wow.'

'I know,' said Mum. 'What a load of old nonsense but … *wow*. Then he said something about bringing "tokens of his regret which should not be taken as acceptance of responsibility". Slimy so-and-so. That means you're getting presents, Billy. Good stuff. All I've got to do is sign a piece of paper saying we're not going to take it to the newspapers or to court or anything, and you get the good gear from Danny Cash. Do you want the good gear or do you want to take it to court?'

'The good gear, of course,' I said. 'What do you think it'll be? Maybe more match tickets?'

That's when a nurse put her head through the curtain around my bed and said, 'You've got some visitors, Billy.'

The nurse disappeared but it wasn't Danny Cash that had come to see me. It was his brother and Mia. She had a box of Celebrations on her lap.

'Hi Billy. Blimey, look at the state of your face,'

she said. 'This is my dad, Owen. Dad, this is Billy and his mum.' She gave me the Celebrations and smiled at my mum.

'Thanks, Mia. Hi, Owen.'

'Alright Billy? Alright Billy's Mum?' said Owen Cash. He sounded just like his brother and looked quite like him too but way more friendly. 'Sorry about Our Danny, he can be a right git sometimes but he means well. How are you feeling, lad?'

'Better than you look, I hope,' said Mia.

'Mia,' said her dad, squatting down beside her. 'We've talked about putting your brain in gear before opening your mouth, haven't we?'

She looked at him, then back at me. 'I'm only kidding, Billy,' she said. 'It's just bruising, yeah? It'll go down in a few days.'

'I've got a broken nose, as well,' I said. 'Your brother knows how to kick a ball, doesn't he?'

'Yeah. He can't do a lot else but he can certainly do that. I used to be pretty good myself but I've got summat way more important in my life now,' said Mia's dad, putting his arm around her shoulders and kissing her cheek. I wished I could do that.

The nurse's disembodied head appeared through the curtain again, 'More visitors, Billy.' Then she mouthed, 'It's Danny Cash!'

She pulled the curtains back to reveal Mr Lusty-Prune, sorry, Lustig-Prean, a photographer, a cameraman and an astonished-looking Danny Cash.

He said, 'Mia, Owen! What the … what on earth are you doing here?'

He looked at me, lying in bed and not looking deeply upset at all. 'Oh hell, not this one again.'

Apparently he hadn't bothered to find out who's face he had mashed up. Mr Lustig-Prean put his hands on the footballer's shoulders and urgently whispered something.

Danny Cash smiled, unconvincingly.

'I'm sorry,' he said. 'It's Willy, isn't it? I didn't know it was you that had … got in the way.'

There was another whisper from Mr Lustig-Prean, who then motioned for the photographer and the cameraman to get to work.

'Where's me manners,' said Danny Cash. 'Mrs Turpin?' he said to my mum – she hates being called 'Mrs' and his accent made our name sound more like one of those little turtles. 'Mrs Turpin, hi, I'm Danny Cash. I'm really sorry for what happened to your son. It was just one of those silly accidents.'

He shook my mum's hand. Then there were hugs and hellos for Mia and her dad. Mia didn't look like she wanted hugging. Her dad called him 'Danny-lad'. It was so crowded the cameraman and the photographer couldn't get any good shots. Mr Lustig-Prean started looking agitated.

'People, people,' he said. 'This is all very touching but we need to get moving here. If we could clear the unnecessary…' He looked at Mia nervously, '…If we could just have Willy and Danny in shot.'

'It's Billy,' said my mum. 'His name is Billy.'

'I *think* that's what I just said,' said Mr Lusty-Prune. 'Now, if we can just get all the flots and jets *behind* the cameras … thankyou thankyou thankyou…'

He handed Danny Cash a holdall and motioned for us all to be quiet. The cameraman gave him a thumbs-up. Danny Cash walked up to me with an apologetic smile and sat down on the edge of my bed.

'Willy…' he said.

'It's Billy,' I said.

'Oh for…'

'Let's try that one again, people,' said Mr Lustig-Prean.

Danny Cash stood up, rolling his eyes towards the ceiling. He walked away, reset his apologetic smile, walked back and sat down again on the edge of my bed.

'Billy,' he said. 'I'm really sorry you got hurt, mate. I got you some stuff that I hope will make you feel better.'

I saw Mr Lustig-Prean behind the camera, pushing a clipboard with a piece of paper on it, under my mum's nose, handing her a pen and showing her where to sign.

Danny Cash reached into the holdall and produced a football.

'This is the one that hit you, W … Billy. I've signed it, here look, and so have the other lads: Carlos, Nicky, Tunje, Alessandro, Muzzy, all of them.'

'Wow,' I said, taking the ball and staring at it stupidly through my bruised and swollen eyelids.

'And here's an Earl's Court baseball cap. I've written on it look: "Never take your eye off the ball – Danny Cash". It's sound advice that.'

He put the cap on my head.

'And here's a pair of season tickets. They're valid for the rest of the season, Billy; every home game. You can bring your mum along.'

'I want to bring Mia, Danny. She's my…' Girlfriend? Special friend? '…she's my best friend. Is that alright?'

He looked at Mr Lustig-Prean who nodded vigorously. Mia gave me the best smile yet.

'Yeah, no probs,' said Danny Cash, standing up. 'I need to go now, mate. The gaffer doesn't like it if you're late for training.'

He shook my hand. The camera flashed for the last

time. Mr Lusty-Prune said, 'Thank you, lovely people; you bring tears to my eyes.'

There was a flurry of handshakes and hugs and goodbyes and the Danny Cash Show swept out of Ward 8. I sat there in my blue and yellow cap, with my black and yellow eyes, my season tickets and my signed football, not quite knowing what to think.

A bit later the doctor looked at me again and said it was fine to go home; just watch out for nausea and dizziness. My nose wasn't actually crooked and would just have to fix itself, she said.

At home I went straight to bed; I was shattered. Nettle's not allowed to sleep on our beds but I let her just this once. We curled up together. The last thing I said to her before closing my eyes, was, 'Do you think he's really sorry, Net?'

She licked my chin and made an awful smell. I fell asleep anyway and dreamed I was running around Wembley Stadium with the Champions League trophy held aloft. Rio was one of my teammates. Nettle was another. I woke up with a wet nose in my ear – Nettle's, thank goodness.

My mum came in and said, 'Do you want a hand getting up, love?'

I let her help me into my wheelchair but I went to the toilet and did everything else by myself. Mum walked Nettle, and I logged on to my laptop and went straight to my socials: **razberi**. Fourteen people had posted, but the name that leapt out at me was **H-bom**. They'd written:

hey billy the flid – check out youtube – spaz getting mashed by football – real funny – check out dan cash mouthin off bout it in club after – even funnier lol – we gonna play sum rasberryball tomorrow bruv – ya get me – ha ha ha ha ha ha ha

14.

Ugly Men

There's a lot of funny videos on YouTube; I spend ages looking at them, laughing at them, chatting about them with my (virtual) friends. Some of them aren't so funny although some people seem to think they are. It's the mean stuff that brings the real saddos out. You read the comments they leave and you wonder what sort of people they must be. Ordinary people, I guess. That's what's scary.

There were four posted versions of me being hit by the football and they had thousands of views already. One of them showed the moment of impact and me falling backwards out of my chair, again and again. It played that old Britney Spears song that goes 'Hit Me Baby One More Time', then showed me getting smacked in the face. Then it showed me unconscious on the ground and Danny Cash laughing with 'Oops, I Did It Again' as the soundtrack. That was the version that had the most hits and the most comments. Stuff like:

its ok – he can walk it off – LOL

and

HAHAHAHAHAHAHAHAHAHAHAHAHA

and

got the raspberry Danny C, wot a star!

and

got what he deserve –
lets kick mongs outta football

…and loads more. I couldn't believe it. These people seemed to really hate me. Complete strangers. I found myself with tears running down my cheeks. I've never felt so angry. I didn't think I even *did* angry. What would Mia do? She'd be furious. Then she'd post some scary reply and not waste any more energy on them. I didn't post any reply but I decided I should be feeling sorry for them, as well as being angry. I'm stuck with my cerebral palsy. These people were *choosing* to be like this.

Then it got worse. I searched for *danny cash* –

nightclub and immediately found a clip entitled, 'Danny Cash invents awesome new game'. I clicked – and wished I hadn't.

It was dark and grainy and clearly shot on a mobile. I suppose it was in a nightclub but I've never been to one. It had been taken on Saturday night, after the game. When I was in hospital. There were three Earl's Court players there: Danny Cash, Alessandro Varice and Nicky Dulgence, wearing really nice, expensive-looking clothes. There was a giggle of glamour girls with them, really dressed up. I recognised one of them: Connie Tempt. She does modelling and reality TV and stuff. She always goes out with footballers. She was all over Danny Cash (like a cheap suit, as my nan would have said) laughing at everything he said. Like any of it was funny.

They all had glasses in their hands and were clearly – thanks again, Nan – three sheets to the wind. There was a load of empty Champagne bottles behind them. Danny Cash spoke and everyone else listened.

'…and the next thing I know, Gary's telling me I've knocked some raspberry out of his wheelchair. As if my life isn't difficult enough, without _____ raspberries cluttering up the place…'

Did I mention that Danny Cash cusses a bit? I just can't tell you everything he said because of all the swear words. Bad ones.

'...I mean, what a ____. All he had to do was move his flamin' head six inches to the side but no, he's gotta give me a hard time, hasn't he? It ain't my ____ fault if he can't get out the way, is it? Next thing I know, I've got the ref giving me a yellow card, half the crowd booing me whenever I touch the ball and the Reverend Gary Lineker on *Match of the Day*, telling everyone I'm the Antichrist or summat. What a ____.'

Now imagine peals of girly laughter after each horrible sentence that comes out of his mouth.

'...then you get Alan flamin' Shearer, St Alan of Gateshead – yeah right – saying how I gotta give up the England captaincy. What a ____.'

Nicky Dulgence said, 'You got that raspberry a beauty, mind. Sweet. Talk about getting what's coming. You blasted him clean out of his wheelchair.'

'Ah mate,' said Danny Cash, gulping down £200 worth of Champagne. 'That was my best shot of the season. I reckon I've invented a new game: Raspberryball.'

The footballers and the ladies dissolved into a mess of giggling. I made plans to take down the rest of my Danny Cash pictures when I'd finished watching. It felt like someone had tipped horse manure all over my life.

'...alright, here's how it goes. If you kick the ball

and hit a raspberry, it's ten points. If you knock it over, it's twenty, and if it needs medical treatment, it's thirty. Seven games to go in the season and I'm thirty points up already, lads. Who's in for a grand, winner takes all?'

'And,' said Nicky Dulgence, 'gets to lift the FA Cup.'

'Eh?'

'The Flid Association.'

'Sick. Nice one,' said Alessandro Varice. The footballers all high-fived and embraced and laughed.

That's when the video ended; a still shot of three drunk, ugly men.

My heroes.

'Come here, Net,' I said and the little hairball sprang up onto my lap and immediately curled up. 'I'm not a raspberry or a flid or a spacker or a spaz, Nettle; I'm a person. But if they call me that stuff, they can pretend I'm not. It's not on, and I'm sorry I swore at you that time. I'm never gonna swear again.' I rubbed her belly and felt the tears come into my eyes. I felt smaller.

Mia. I didn't know how she would react to this so I figured I'd send her a text. It seemed safer.

'**Billy's phone – MESSAGE**.' The voice recognition kicked in. My mobile lit up and highlighted the address field. '**To MIA**.' I said, then started to dictate.

'Hi. Have a look at your Uncle Danny in the nightclub posted online,' I said. 'Mia, it's sickening. I'm sorry but forget about the football in the face. This makes me feel like I've had my guts ripped out. Emoji: kiss. **Billy's phone – SEND**'.

The reply came back almost immediately.

> *Don't be sorry. Seen it. Can't believe it.*
> *I'll kill him. So sorry Billy. XX*

I stared at my mobile. 'It's gotta be embarrassing for her, Nettle,' I said to the sleeping dog. 'It's her uncle after all. Or her dad.'

Nettle didn't stir but an evil smell drifted up from her tiny body.

'Thanks for your input, Net. You're a great help.'

She growled gently as I eased her to the floor. I wiped my eyes and started taking my remaining Danny Cash pictures down. All fifteen of them. I had more that I needed to say to Mia but I had to get my thoughts together. One picture left: it was the signed one that all the kids had been given when the footballers visited school. It seemed like ages ago. It followed the others into the bin.

'**Billy's phone – REPLY**. There's something else, Mia,' I dictated. 'I got another threatening message from H-Bom. He said they're gonna play raspberryball with me tomorrow. It has to be someone from our class. It's gotta be Rio. It seems like they all hate me even more since I won those tickets. I thought it would make them like me, Mia. I don't know what to do. Emoji: kiss. **Billy's phone – SEND.'**

I hated sounding so helpless to Mia. All I really wanted to do was to impress her, but I just felt like crying. I felt like asking my mum or Mrs Welbeck to sort it all out for me. Like they always used to. Nettle glared at me and growled from under my desk.

'Great,' I said. 'So, you hate me too.'

'Billy, your tea's ready,' shouted my mum from the kitchen.

'Coming,' I said. Nettle stayed in her cave.

It was egg on toast. With beans on top, and brown sauce. It was OK, Mum hadn't managed to ruin it. Oh, and Mike was there. He was a bit nervous but we managed to chat about football and my broken nose. He supports Leyton Orient. I guess someone has to do it. He didn't seem so bad; I think he likes me. He even made me laugh a couple of times and as long as he makes my mum happy … I suppose he's got to be alright.

When I got back to my room, there was a text (and a dog) waiting for me. I called Nettle back onto my lap and pulled up to my desk to read Mia's message. It said:

right. I don't care if he's blood. That bloomin lowlife danny cash has gone too far and so has H-bom. If they want to play, we'll show them how to play. Meet me by the gym before registration tomorrow. We're gonna make plans. XX

'Oh Gawd, Nettle,' I said. 'She wants to take them all on. Do *I* want to take them all on?'

Nettle eyed me intensely as I spoke. When I stopped, she sneezed onto my special keyboard. Her wet black nose left a little slug trail on a single key. The same letter that appeared on my screen. The letter,

Y.

OK then. Time to take on the world, I guess.

15.

My First High-Five

'Anything good happening at school today?' said Mike over breakfast – a bowl of cereal and a glass of orange juice, no bits. Not even *my mum* can ruin that. Mia said she has to make her own breakfast. And cook the evening meal when she gets back from school.

'Maybe,' I said. 'I think so. I hope so. I don't know. I've got this … person to deal with. Kind of a bully.'

'A bully? Billy, what's happening? You never mentioned a bully,' said my mum, stopping her clattering at the sink. 'Right, I'm not having it – I'll speak to Mr Balotelli. Who is it?'

'I'm dealing with it, Mum,' I said. 'Me and Mia are dealing with it.'

'What do you mean you're dealing with it, Billy? You're both vulnerable,' said Mum.

'…and so, we can't do anything for ourselves?'

'I didn't say that.'

'You didn't have to,' I said. 'We're dealing with it.'

'OK, your mum's naturally concerned and you

136

need to keep her up to speed, Billy,' said Mike. 'If you need any help, just ask: me, your mum, any adult you trust at school … it can seem like you're very alone, when bad stuff like this is happening, but you're not. Never. And hats off for dealing with this … thing … person … whatever it is. I'm sure it's not easy.'

'Billy…'

'Mum, if I can't handle it, I'll tell you, OK? Me and Mia are good together. We'll deal with it.'

Mum and Mike exchanged glances, then Mum came over and gave me a hug.

'I'm sure you can deal with it, babes, but like Mike says, remember you're not alone.'

She kissed me on the cheek and left a little slug trail, just like Nettle's nose does.

'Mu-um…' I said, wiping my cheek, but it felt good really.

❦

Mia was waiting for me when I got to the gym entrance. I get the 'special' bus into school but she gets a lift from her dad and she'd clearly got in early.

'Blimey, Billy,' she said, looking at the time on her mobile. 'What were you doing, pushing the bus in?'

'Hi Mia,' I said. 'It's good to see you too.'

She smiled and said, 'Billy, we gotta sort this out. I

don't know what the hell to do with my Uncle Danny, pondlife that he is, but I got a plan for H-bom.'

'Rio.'

'Probably. Look, have you deleted those messages you got from him, like I told you?'

I hadn't. I thought she might be angry.

'No,' I said. 'I'm still deciding what to do.'

'Brill. Billy, I need your login details. Is that alright? I won't take the mick. I need your login name and password. You can always change it after. We've got IT after break, haven't we? Listen, if it's alright with you, I'm gonna have a word with Miss Savage…'

Miss Savage is our IT teacher. She has long blonde hair and a lovely Welsh accent. Most of the boys say they fancy her. Rio reckons *she* fancies *him*. He would. She doesn't. Miss Savage is alright but she goes on a bit. Especially about cyber-bullying. She talks about it forever, then makes us discuss it: how we *feeeel* about it. I think that just gives people ideas, but she means well.

Mia told me her plan and it was awesome. I was so excited by it; I was shaking even more than usual as we rolled into registration together.

Mr Balotelli wasn't quite ready. 'Good morning, Mia. Good morning, Billy,' he said. 'Find a … find a space.'

You're not allowed to bring balls into class. You have to keep them in your bag until break but Rio had a football in his hands anyway. He stared at me with an unpleasant grin on his face and bounced the ball on the floor between his feet, catching it without looking, without taking his eyes off me. Rio really hates me. My mind flashed back to primary school: Rio sitting on my lap as we hurtled in my wheelchair down the path leading up to school, both screaming with excitement. We hadn't thought it through; we hit a parked car at the bottom and did some damage. We got into SO MUCH TROUBLE over that. For weeks afterwards, Rio only had to look at me and we would both snort with laughter, giggle for ages. I used to love laughing with Rio.

'OK, everybody,' said Mr Balotelli. 'When you're ready. Rio, you need to put your football away right now, please.'

'It ain't my ball, sir,' said Rio and he threw it to Hisham, but in such a way that he couldn't possibly catch it.

The ball spilled onto the floor and started bouncing around, off desks and kids' legs. Some of the kids gave it a little kick to keep it going.

'Pick the ball up, please,' said Mr Balotelli, moving towards it and bending down.

Just before he reached it, Tyrell kicked the ball away from his hands and it started bouncing around behind him. Kids were beginning to laugh and shout.

'Sorry, sir,' said Tyrell. 'I was trying to get it to you.'

'Somebody, pick the ball up please,' said Mr Balotelli, going very red.

It rolled to Yakubu who trapped it under his foot and picked it up.

'There you go, sir,' said Yakubu, handing it to Mr Balotelli.

There was booing.

'Thank you, Yakubu. I think perhaps I need to confiscate this ball…'

'Sir, that ain't fair,' said Hisham. 'It's my ball and I never done nothing.'

Mr Balotelli looked defeated already and it was only nine o'clock. 'Hisham,' he said after a pause. 'Put the ball away now or lose it until the end of the day.'

'Yes, sir.'

Hisham grinned at me as he walked out with the football and he bounced it right next to my chair, before catching it again.

At break, Mia went off to talk to Miss Savage and I went to the library. It was the only place I felt safe. I didn't fancy a game of raspberryball.

Although they don't have a keyboard I can use, I

can manage the mouse. So I went onto the computer and checked if there were any more messages from H-bom. There weren't, but while I was looking, I started to get an idea on how to handle the Danny Cash situation. It meant turning the virtual into the real. It meant being stupidly brave again. I wasn't certain I could muster the courage but I reckoned Raz Beri probably could.

When the bell went for the end of break, my heart leapt inside my chest. Mia and Miss Savage were already in the IT room. So were most of the class. Mia mouthed, 'It's OK.'

'Right,' said Miss Savage. 'A change of plan today. I want you to start with ten minutes free time on the computers, during which I want you to research how secure we are online: are we really private when we search and message and virtually interact? Can we be traced by others? You can work by yourselves, in pairs or in groups. I'll be coming around to see how all of you are doing.'

The kids all sorted themselves out. In the usual way since starting secondary school. I made my way, alone, to a computer. One of the old ones that takes forever. Most kids were in pairs or threes. The biggest group was centred on (The Evil) Rio: they were (Lame-Brain) Liam, ('Orrible) Orla, (Loathsome) Luca and

(Horrible) Hisham. They were soon laughing and pointing at the screen.

Mia had positioned herself at Miss Savage's keyboard, the one that controls what happens on the big interactive whiteboard that the whole class can see.

'Hey, H-bom,' called Mia, out of the blue.

Hisham's head shot around to look at her, a mixture of surprise and annoyance on his face.

'Well, that was just *too* easy,' said Mia, left-clicking Miss Savage's mouse. A message appeared on the interactive whiteboard. I'd read it before. It said:

hey billy the flid – check out youtube – spaz gettting mashed by football – real funny – check out dan cash mouthin off bout it in club after – even funnier lol – we gonna play sum rasberyball tomorrow bruv – ya get me – ha ha ha ha ha ha ha

'Where's your football, H-bom?' said Mia. 'You can play some raspberryball with me if you like. If you're brave enough.'

Rio quickly leant over and whispered something to Hisham who said, 'I ain't H-bom. I don't know nothing about H-bom.'

'OK, Mr Bom, sorry, Hisham,' said Mia, left-clicking Miss Savage's mouse again. The whiteboard changed to another familiar message. It didn't look half so scary now that it was out in the open.

who dya fink u r spaz? yer ded meat bruv. ya get me?

'That ain't me,' said Hisham. 'I never said that.'

'These threatening messages,' said Miss Savage, 'were sent to Billy, our friend and classmate. Almost certainly by someone in this room. Does anybody have an opinion on them? Please feel free to speak up.'

I held my breath. Would my classmates finally support me?

Rio started glaring around at all the kids. Miss Savage casually moved over and stood in front of him.

'No one's pointing a finger at anyone,' said Miss Savage. 'Just hypothetically, what do you think of these threatening messages?'

Lots of the kids were looking down. Some looked at me. Some looked at Rio and Hisham. After a short while, Maysoon put her hand up.

'Yes, Maysoon.'

'I think they're horrible, miss.'

'Thank you, Maysoon. Anyone else?'

Three more hands went up. Four. Six. Nine.

Precious said, 'It's sad, miss. People who send messages like this need to get a life.'

Sakinah said, 'This stuff can ruin people's lives.'

Junaid said, 'It's just cowards that hide behind a computer screen or a tablet or a mobile, miss. It's pathetic.'

Eboni said, 'These people are scum, miss. I get loads of stuff like this as well. Texts and stuff. I ain't never told before but I'm sick of their chattin' – sick of being scared.'

Miss Savage thanked her and said they would talk after class.

Umehabibah said, 'It's just bullying, miss. Same as getting bullied in the playground.'

Over half my tutor group had something to say. Even some of the boys. Speaking up for me! My heart was pounding against my ribs. I wanted to cry with happiness.

When they had finished, Miss Savage said, 'Thank you everybody. That was outstanding. I'll be passing on everything you have said to Mr Balotelli and to Mr Hodgson. In future, I'd like you to know that if anyone is sending you inappropriate messages online or via mobile or however, this is a place it will be dealt with. Also, to anyone sending *any* message of any sort, bear in mind that you can be traced via your ISP. Threatening messages are not just offensive, they are

144

an offence and if we can't deal with them in school, we can always go to the police.'

There was a silence, but it was like her words were echoing in the room.

'I didn't want to do it,' Hisham blurted. 'Rio made me, miss.'

'I never. You're a liar,' said Rio.

That's when things got nasty. Miss Savage had to step between them.

Mia said, 'Do you wanna tell Miss Savage about what happened to you in the woods?'

'After the lesson,' I replied.

It felt safer with just me and Miss Savage in the room, and now Hisham and Rio were in so much trouble. They were given appointments to meet with our headteacher, Mr Hodgson, along with their parents. That's proper trouble. Hisham had his football confiscated and Mr Balotelli said he was not allowed to bring one in again this term. Get you Mr B!

At dinnertime, Mia raised her hand and we high-fived. My first high-five! First successful one anyhow. I tried one once with my mum but we missed.

When we'd finished eating, Mrs Welbeck asked me if I needed the toilet.

I said, 'Yes, but I can manage, thanks, Mrs Welbeck.'

She looked hurt, but I had said it politely. Mia wanted to high-five again but it seemed rude so I didn't.

In the playground afterwards, Mia said, 'Spaz 1, Bag 0.'

'Can you stop calling me that?' I said. 'I don't like it.'

'I'm sorry. I was joking. I'll even stop calling The Bag "The Bag" if you can figure out what to do about my bloomin' Uncle Danny.'

'Oh, I've got a plan for him,' I said. 'I've got an awesome plan. Come Sunday, Uncle Danny is going to learn that we're people too, but this time I really am gonna need some help.'

I don't know what's got into me these days, but these words keep coming out of my mouth. No turning back now.

16.

My Second Match

Manchester United. Another massive game for Earl's Court this Sunday. At this stage of the season, they come thick and fast. It was live on Sky at four o'clock. Half the world was going to be watching. Me and Mia were going to be there. Pitch-side, just behind the advertising hoardings.

I'd been busy all week on my laptop. Or rather, Raz Beri had. I like Raz; he seems braver than me. Rio and Hisham had got what was coming to them and now Danny Cash was going to as well. It was time the world saw what Billy Turpin is really made of.

Nettle had been way less demanding. She seemed content to watch me as I worked away online. I concentrated on my London Disabled forum. There were loads of Earl's Court fans there, loads of fans of other clubs and loads of people who don't care about football at all, but there was one thing that united them all. They were all, every last one of them, *furious* about the Danny Cash incident and what he had said in that club. They were spitting feathers, as my nan would have said. They wanted to DO SOMETHING. And they were going to get their chance in the forty-fourth minute of Earl's Court's home game against Manchester United. Raz was going to see to it.

I never dreamt that my second match would come around so fast and I never dreamt that it could be even more dramatic than my first. How scary is that? The big difference was that this time, *I* was making things happen.

School had been alright, I suppose. I'd been treading water to be honest (I know, I know. You pretty much *have* to understand metaphor if you're disabled), just waiting for Sunday. The best thing was that Rio and Hisham were in *so much trouble*: they were on Headteacher's Report and one sneeze out of place and they would be excluded. They just left me alone really, apart from giving me dirty looks and I could cope with that alright. Apparently I can cope with loads of things these days. Rio took the mick out of my voice once when none of the teachers could hear, but do you know what? I didn't care.

I just stared at him and said, 'If it makes you happy, Rio, but it isn't *me* that sounds stupid'.

Most of Rio's 'friends' were ignoring him and Hisham, and some people were even being nice to *me*. Now that *was* a bit hard to cope with. That hadn't happened since primary school and to be honest, it felt pretty darn good. What felt best of all though, was that I was learning not to care what people like Rio and Danny Cash said. They're sad, small people who need to grow up.

I so wanted to tell my classmates what was happening on Sunday but I just couldn't risk it. Only Mia knew. We spent every break huddled together, planning, scheming. Huddlage is good. I like huddling with Mia. Everyone at school would be watching the match: me and Mia had told them something incredible was going to happen and that they had to watch. It was SO hard not saying any more but we couldn't risk being found out.

When Sunday came, Mia's dad dropped us off near the ground at the end of Easi-Noodle Boulevard. Our parents weren't at all sure about us going by ourselves, but we said we really needed to be independent. We insisted. It wasn't a lie. Not really. It just wasn't *quite* the whole truth either.

We started wheeling ourselves towards the huge

yellow and blue stadium. The crowds got thicker the closer we got and everyone was towering over us.

There was a cluster around the life-size bronze statue of Simon Cowell; they were like ants around a caterpillar. Some fans like to touch it for luck before going into the ground. I couldn't believe where most of them were touching him! We joined the cluster and put up with being buffeted while we waited for our turn. For *my* turn, at least. Mia said she doesn't believe in luck *or* Simon Cowell so she wasn't going to bother, but she stuck with me anyway and I figured we were going to need all the help we could get. I put my hand on his cold, cold shin. I couldn't reach any higher. I felt a little stronger but fear still wriggled its fingers.

Inside the ground, the atmosphere was even better than the Chelsea game. The United fans were in good voice and so was the home crowd. They were trying to drown each other out. I didn't join in. I was looking to see how many wheelchair users had turned up. A lot, and plenty that I hadn't seen there last time. I figured that these must be my 'virtual' friends but now they were flesh and blood. It was a warm day but none of them were just in T-shirts; they were all covered up, like me. This was a good sign.

The famous old digital clock in the Nelson

Mandela Stand clicked onto **3:59**. The players took their positions. The referee looked at his watch. The United fans sang, 'You know what you are. You know what you are-re-re. Oh, Danny Cash, you know what you are.'

He didn't look happy. The ref blew his whistle and the game began.

4:11: It was good stuff. Both teams created chances but nobody put one away. Danny Cash was booed every time he touched the ball and it didn't sound like it was just coming from the United fans. I looked at Mia and she was miles away. She looked scared, vulnerable. I wanted to put my hand on hers, to give her a hug. She saw me looking and the confident smile came back.

'Alright, Superman?' she said.

4:27: Nicky Dulgence messed up a good chance and the jeering went on for ages. It sounded like drunken crows on the loose. He aimed an extremely unpleasant gesture towards the United fans and the referee had a word. The jeering got worse.

4:39: Five minutes to go. The game settled into a stalemate and the crowd quietened down. You could hear some individual shouts from fans, mostly aimed at Danny Cash, some at Nicky Dulgence and Alessandro Varice. None of them nice.

4:43: Both teams now playing for half-time. I unzipped my jacket and looked over at Mia. My insides were in knots. I was sweating. I couldn't do this.

Mia smiled and mouthed, 'It's OK.' Then she said out loud, 'What's the worst that can happen?' and coolly shrugged.

It's nice getting the approval of others but it's more important to do the right thing. I smiled back.

Mia moved down to the other end of the advertising hoarding that we were behind. I tried not to think about the worst thing that could happen. So many options and none of them good.

Manchester United were passing the ball around in midfield without committing anyone forward to try to score. Earl's Court held their shape. I held my breath and let my jacket fall to the ground. I must be mad.

I'd spent hours with a permanent marker on my T-shirt. It seemed like a game at the time. My best white T-shirt. Mum was going to kill me. It read:

I'M NO RASPBERRY. SAY HELLO TO RAZ BERI

4:44: Mia revealed her T-shirt too. It felt like insanity but we started wheeling ourselves onto the pitch. I was sure that the stewards would stop us but they just didn't know what to do. I don't think they wanted to be seen manhandling wheelchair users so they did nothing.

One of them shouted, 'YOU, get back here.'

But we ignored him. I don't know if I've ever ignored a grown-up before.

I felt like I was wheeling myself off a cliff but it was amazing because all along the sidelines, there were other wheelchair users stripping off their jumpers and jackets and making their way onto the pitch, just like we'd been planning all week. Young and old, male and female, Black, white and brown. Thirty, forty, sixty, one hundred wheelchairs rolled onto the turf. More than the stewards could ever deal with. The players stopped running. The ball was kicked into touch. Some of the stewards were shouting into their walkie-talkies. The referee blew his whistle, for no obvious reason.

All the protesters had slogans on their shirts, like me. Some printed properly, some scrawled in black marker. Many of them on expensive Earl's Court and Manchester United replica shirts.

I'M A PERSON, NOT A RASPBERRY

My Name is EDITH

My name is Dipak – A PERSON

I'M A HUMAN BEING – HOW ABOUT YOU DANNY CASH?

MY NAME IS STANLEY

MY NAME IS IRENKA

I'M a mother, a wife, a friend, a smoker, a Man U fan, a receptionist, a woman – NOT a raspberry

MY NAME IS WINSTON – I AM A MAN

CALL ME WHAT YOU LIKE DANNY – AT LEAST I'M NOT A BIGOT

Mia's T-shirt read:

MY NAME IS MIA – WHO'S THE DADDY?

The players' path to the tunnel was blocked. They looked uncertain and started forming small groups in the centre of the pitch. We moved in, in a circle, herding them together. The crowd went silent. Totally silent. Forty-five thousand people have never been so quiet. All eyes turned to me. Always my worst nightmare. I remembered the cameras, the millions watching, worldwide. Mum and Mike would be watching, my classmates, Mr Marsh, Owen Cash, Mr Balotelli, Nettle... I wondered what the Sky Sports commentators would be saying. And I realised that I didn't care. I gathered my deepest reserves of courage and maturity, put my tongue between my lips, and blew. I blew a raspberry at the bewildered, multimillionaires in front of me. A single, solitary raspberry that pierced the silence of the Wang's Tofu Arena like a poppy growing through concrete.

Mia followed suit. And Winston. And Stanley. And Irenka. And Dipak. And Edith. And all the other wheelchair users, young and old, male and female, Black, white and brown. And we didn't stop. Some people in the crowd joined in: Manchester United fans, Earl's Court fans. More and more, hundreds, then thousands, then tens of thousands. Forty-five thousand people joined together in the world's greatest ever raspberry.

It sounded like nothing this planet has heard before. The very air became wet; the sound came in vast pulses, shaking the ground and vibrating the stands in damp, rhythmic throbs. Children covered their ears, a sound man from Sky Sports cuddled his furry microphone, trying to shield it from the sonic onslaught. Some of the footballers looked panicked, some just folded their arms. I think Gary Reed was actually joining in. Danny Cash looked straight at Mia with an expression I'd never seen on his face before.

And I stopped. It was enough. I turned my wheelchair around and started heading back to my place behind the advertising hoarding. Mia followed, as did Winston and Stanley and Irenka and Dipak and Edith and all the other wheelchair users. The monstrous raspberry that shook West London, quickly turned into a slightly moist memory.

There was still a minute plus stoppage time left in the first half but the referee blew for half-time anyway and pointed to the tunnel. The players mostly looked down at the ground, but you could see their relief as they jogged off the pitch in the silent arena.

I thought I would be arrested or chucked out of the ground at least, but no one did a thing. We all returned to our places while the stewards looked the other way and pretended nothing had happened.

We'd done it. Raz Beri had done it. *I'd* done it. I looked at Mia and I could see she was buzzing. I guess I was too. Mia's face was alive with adrenaline, with excitement.

'Oh-My-God,' she said, with her eyes open wide. '*That* was AWESOME.' And she spread her arms to give me the hug that I'd been dreaming of since I first saw her.

I moved my wheelchair around and opened my arms wide too, just as Mr Lustig-Prean arrived with a huge, yellow-jacketed steward with cropped hair. Instead of my fantasy hug, I experienced the familiar lurch of fear in my stomach. Lustig-Prean pointed at me and Mia with a stoney face.

'Those two,' he said.

17.

The Raz Beri Foundation

The steward with the cropped hair moved towards us while Mr Lustig-Prean looked on. I noticed a pitch-side camera was trained on us.

'Excuse me, miss,' said the big man in the fluorescent yellow jacket. 'Mr Cash would like a word. You too, sir, if you wouldn't mind.'

Miss? Sir? I was so far out of my comfort zone; I didn't know what was going on. Maybe this was what it was like when you get in trouble in the big wide world. *Serious* trouble, not just school trouble. Maybe they start off being really polite before they take you somewhere that no one else can see and … and what? What do they do to you when you mess up in the grown-up world? What was Danny Cash going to do? Something awful with his monstrous thighs? Would Mr Lustig-Prean join in? Nicky Dulgence? Alessandro Varice?

'This way please, miss, sir,' said the steward. 'Would you like us to push you?'

At least he asked.

'No thanks,' said Mia. 'We can manage. Where are we going?'

'We're just going to follow Mr Lustig-Prean. I think he's going to the Press Room.'

The Press Room? That didn't sound so scary. Lusty-Prune looked like a man with a mouthful of wasps but the steward seemed quite nice. They led us along the side of the pitch and down the players' tunnel. Wow! I didn't care what happened to us; we were going down the players' tunnel! It smelled of that stuff they rub into their legs at half-time. I wondered if it would help my legs any.

'There you go, miss,' said the big steward.

They'd taken us to a room with several rows of chairs in it. It looked a bit like a classroom except that at one end there were microphones on the tables and sponsors' logos on the walls. I recognised it. I'd seen it a hundred times. It was where they do the post-match press conferences.

The steward left us so it was just me and Mia, alone with Mr Lustig-Prean. He didn't look happy. There was a long silence.

'What happens now, Mr Lustig-Prean? Sorry, Seb,' said Mia.

'Mr Lustig-Prean to you, I think. Danny Cash will

be out in a minute. Thanks to your little prank, he's in no state to play the second half. He's being substituted. I hope you're pleased with yourselves.'

Lustig-Prean glared at us in a silence that lasted a minute or two but felt more like twenty. I looked down, of course. Mia stared him out, of course. We heard the crowd greet the players coming out onto the pitch for the second half.

The door opened and Danny Cash came through, wearing an Earl's Court tracksuit over his playing kit. He looked different, smaller. The arrogance had gone. He attempted a smile. Not successfully.

'Alright, kids,' he said, sitting himself on a plastic chair in front of us, elbows on knees.

'Hi, Uncle Danny,' said Mia.

'Hi, Danny,' I said, wondering what was coming next. Would this be where the bad stuff really started?

'That was quite a stunt you pulled out there,' said Danny Cash. 'And I had it coming. Fair play to you.'

I didn't know what to say.

'It looked like you two were the ringleaders, am I right?'

'It was me,' I blurted, which was true but, also, I didn't want Mia getting into trouble. 'I organised it.'

Lustig-Prean nodded with a scowl on his face.

'Well, Willy, it seems like you're one hell of an organiser,' said Danny Cash.

'Thank you, and it's Billy,' I said.

Danny Cash slumped in his chair looking like a pricked balloon. He rubbed his thinning hair and said, 'Of course it is. Well, Billy, like I say, I had it coming. I really asked for it and what I wanna say more than anything, is that I'm sorry. Not because some PR man has told me to, not just to look good on the cameras. I behaved like a complete burk and I'm genuinely sorry. Hitting you in the face with that ball was an accident but I shouldn't have acted like a toddler in the first place, and then saying all that stuff in the club … I've watched it back and I can hardly believe it was me. I mean, I was drunk and that but that's no excuse for anything…'

'Let's be clear here,' said Mr Lustig-Prean. 'What Danny is saying is in no way an admission of responsibility…'

'L-P, give it a rest. I *am* responsible. That's what I'm saying here. That's the whole point. Listen L-P, could you leave us for a bit? I need to say what I need to say. Anyway, you gotta write that press statement for me. You know I'm no good at stuff like that. They'll be needing it after the game. Oh, and L-P? Can you make sure that we see Owen as soon as he gets here?'

Lustig-Prean stood up with, as my nan would have said, a face like a slapped arse.

'Be careful what you say, Danny,' he said as he left the room.

'That man's a nightmare,' said Mia, not so quietly. 'Anyway, what do you mean, Owen? Do you mean my dad?'

'Yeah,' said Danny Cash. 'We rang him up; he's coming straight in. He needs to be here for this.'

'What do you mean? What's all this about?'

'When your dad comes, yeah?' said Danny Cash. 'Listen, I'm gonna talk to the press soon but I wanted to say it to you first. You two and your mates have put a mirror up to me and I don't much like what I see. Straight up, I can't live like that. There's gonna be changes, big changes. I know you're angry and you've got every right to be, but I hope I haven't stopped you being fans. Not all footballers are morons like me.'

'I've taken all your pictures down and thrown them away,' I said. 'Sorry, Danny.'

'I don't blame you, Billy-lad, but is there any chance we could shake hands and start again?'

'My hands always shake,' I said, holding them up to show him.

He smiled sadly. 'Well, mine are shaking too right now, mate,' he said, copying my pose to show me.

'How's about we put them together and see if we can help each other out?'

He offered me his hand and I took it. The handshake was firm and steady.

'Nice one, Billy.'

'It's Willy,' I said.

'Oh, for the love of … why can't I get this right?'

'No, it *is* Billy. You were right. I was joking. Sorry.'

'*You* are something else, young man,' said Danny Cash. 'And as for you…'

He turned his attention to Mia, just as there was a knock at the door. It opened immediately.

'Danny,' said Lustig-Prean. 'It's your brother.'

'Thanks L-P.'

Owen Cash walked in without smiling and embraced Mia straight away.

'Mia, I'm so proud of you,' he said. 'And I love you so much.'

'Billy,' said Danny Cash. 'No offence, mate, but could you give us a minute? We got family stuff here. You can watch the rest of the match in that room over there, if you like.'

He pointed to a door at the side. A muffled roar made the walls vibrate. Danny Cash clenched his fist, 'Yes, 1–0. If you're quick, Billy, you can catch the replay. See who scored.'

I was. I did. It was Gary Reed. I thought about telling the others but I knew they had more important stuff to get through. I watched the rest of the game with my brain racing.

My mobile was going crazy: endless calls and texts. I didn't take any of the calls but I looked at a few texts. One from my mum:

Billy love. I'm so proud of you and your nan will be looking down, the proudest woman in heaven. Ring me ASAP babes. X

Loads from my classmates, like this one from Yakubu:

mate u r unbelievable. no ones ever gonna call you bad stuff again

And one that jumped off the screen at me:

bruv its rio – respect mate

Finally. But do you know what? I didn't care what Rio thought of me anymore. I had Mia now. I had self-respect. I didn't need his approval. Maybe he needed mine.

I pictured my nan looking down at me, smiling.

It was a good game but it didn't seem to matter so much. Manchester United equalised in injury time. Of course. The ref blew for full-time and our title chances ended there and then. There's always next season.

After the adverts, they showed the highlights of the game: first the goals, then the wheelchair protest. I watched myself (on telly again!) and the other wheelchair users herding the footballers together. The camera focused on *me*, with my Raz Beri T-shirt and my tongue between my lips. The presenter said that I was thought to be the ringleader and that in an extraordinary development, I was holding talks with Danny Cash.

He said, 'Danny Cash is said to be considering his future.'

'I've considered it,' said Danny Cash, behind me. I hadn't heard him come in. 'Thanks for giving us time, Billy. Are you coming to the press conference? I think you might enjoy it.'

It looked like Mia had been crying but she smiled when she saw me and we sat next to each other, away from the journalists, for the press conference.

Behind the tables, Danny Cash was sitting with Gary Reed, Lusty-Prune and Paolo Di Canio, the Earl's Court manager. The journalists smelled of sweat and alcohol and were all shouting questions. It was like when everybody talks at the same time in class and you can't hear what anyone is saying. Danny Cash stood up and a dozen cameras flashed at once.

'Thanks gents, ladies,' he said. 'I'd like to make a statement now, and you'd best listen carefully, cos I won't be answering any questions afterwards.'

Mr Lustig-Prean, sitting next to Danny, handed him a piece of paper and motioned with his hands for everyone to sit down quietly. Just like school again.

Danny Cash looked at the paper in his hand. He looked at Lusty-Prune, then back at the paper. He turned it in his hands and scanned the other side while the journalists waited expectantly.

'Yeah. I'd like to make a statement, but not this one. I'm sorry, L-P, but this really is a load of rubbish.'

Danny Cash tore the paper into a dozen pieces and let them flutter down onto the table. Lusty-Prune gathered them up and looked nervously at Paolo Di Canio.

Gary Reed smiled and whispered, 'Go on, Danny.'

'My name is Danny Cash and I'm a childish, disrespectful prat…' he began and the journalists listened in stunned silence. 'I wanna start by congratulating those protesters today; you were spot on…'

Danny Cash spoke at length, telling the room everything he had told me and Mia.

I turned to her. 'What did they say in there?' I whispered.

'Oh, nothing much,' she said. 'Just that my Uncle Danny is my real dad and my dad is actually my Uncle Owen and that they've known this for years because they did DNA tests but they never bothered telling me, they just thought we could all live a lie instead.'

'WHAT?' I said. 'I don't believe it.'

Although I did.

Mia smiled sadly. 'It's OK. I just need to get used to the idea of having two dads.'

'How's that gonna work?'

'I know, I know, it's not gonna be easy. I don't know how we're gonna work it out but, the thing is, I know we will. Because we all want to and because people are finally being honest and behaving like adults. I'll keep on living with D... with Owen and I'll keep on calling him Dad, I guess. I don't know, we'll figure it out.'

There was a lot to take in. Danny Cash was still talking.

'So, cos of all this stuff, I'm retiring from international football. It's been a fantastic honour representing my country but I'm no longer available for selection. I want to devote my time to something even more important: my amazing daughter...'

Lusty-Prune sat with his head in his hands.

'I'm also gonna set up a charity. I don't know

exactly how it's gonna work but I'm really excited about it. It's gonna be called…' he looked around and his eyes settled on me, '…the Raz Beri Foundation and it's gonna help disabled kids through sport, not just football. You can do amazing things with horses and martial arts and stuff. Listen, I'm stupidly rich. I'm gonna give, I dunno, ten per cent of my earnings to the Raz Beri Foundation. What's it to me? I'll still have more money than I can ever spend. I'm gonna ask my teammates and other Premier League players to do the same. I think they can spare a few quid. Starting with Nicky and Alessandro; let's be 'aving you, lads.

'Look, I've acted like a burk and this is just my way of showing that I mean it when I say I'm sorry. Oh yeah, and there's a lad called Billy who's taught me a thing or two lately and I was thinking maybe he can help me run The Foundation in a few years' time, if you'll do me the honour, Billy. I think that's it, unless you can think of anything else, L-P?'

Lustig-Prean kept his head in his hands and said nothing.

'No? Oh yeah, in future I'll save me swearing for the ref. Urm, yeah, I'm done. Ta.'

Danny Cash stood up and walked out of the room. Lusty-Prune stood up and said something about 'aspirations, not commitments' but no one heard.

No one was listening anyway. The journalists were going crazy; there was uproar. I figured we would leave them to it. Me and Mia started wheeling ourselves towards the exit. I thought she might be upset but she had the biggest smile lighting up her face. Lighting up my world. We heard clamour behind us, coming our way.

'BILLY!'

'RAZ!'

Before I knew it, we were surrounded. Cameras everywhere, microphones thrust into my face. Lusty-Prune was left talking to the backs of people's heads. One journalist pushed his way to the front. I recognised him; I'd seen him on *Match of the Day*.

'Raz? Raz Beri? Jermaine Jenas from the BBC. Can I ask you some questions, Raz?'

'Sure,' I said. In fact, I squeaked, but who cares? That's just how I talk.

As I listened to his question, I felt no panic about speaking in public, even with all the cameras there. I smiled as I considered my answer and I thought my heart would explode when I felt Mia slip her hand into mine and squeeze.

Matt Stephens lives in Bristol. He derives joy and inspiration from his two daughters and three granddaughters. A turbulent past has been soothed by yoga, meditation and the realisation that human good outweighs human evil. He writes for adults under the name Ed Trewavas and currently works in a major supermarket. Previous employment has included warehouse work, farm labouring and nursery/infant teaching. He enjoys cooking, sport (well, Bristol Rovers) and, most importantly, spending time with family and friends.